TWO CUPIDS
TOO MANY

TWO CUPIDS
TOO MANY

•

Mary Leask

AVALON BOOKS
NEW YORK

PRINTED IN THE UNITED STATES OF AMERICA
ON ACID-FREE PAPER
BY HADDON CRAFTSMEN, BLOOMSBURG, PENNSYLVANIA

This book is dedicated to Jennifer and Don, and Vesta and George;
friends through the years, in good times and in bad,
and
to Dr. Donna Jubb, DVM,
who kindly guided me through the world of veterinary medicine.

Chapter One

Dr. Dan Hamilton eased his Pathfinder in behind the row of cars parked along the country lane. Turning off the engine, he put the window down on the driver's side and leaned back against the SUV's headrest.

He let the quiet of the winter night seep over him. The air was so clear he could almost hear the stars sparkling as they pierced the darkness of the sky. Filling his lungs with the cold crisp air, he felt the tension in his muscles relax.

It had been an exhausting week. It seemed as if every cow, horse, dog and cat in the vicinity of Stewart's Falls had had an emergency. He'd spent more nights in farmers' barns than in his own bed. The bizarre week of early snowstorms and cold temperatures in a time when the world's climate was heating up had added to the strain of rushing through clinic hours and tearing off over the countryside.

But tonight was important to his friends, Carolyn

1

and David Reid, who lived in the newly renovated Victorian farmhouse at the top of the lane. They were celebrating the end of the restoration of the house and the beginning of December and the Christmas season. Bushes outside the house twinkled with fairy lights and long beams of gold poured out through the tall Victorian windows across the snow.

Dan smiled. He remembered the first time that he'd had an inkling that Carolyn and David might someday become a couple. He'd met Carolyn for one of the first tennis games of the season. They were well-matched and usually enjoyed a rather lazy game, not caring who won, just playing for the fun of it. But that night, Carolyn had been nearly dancing with energy, slamming balls back as fast as he could return them. He'd finally called it quits and took her off for coffee in the hope of discovering just what she was so keyed up about. Much to her chagrin, he'd roared with laughter when he heard of the antics of the owner of the house she was starting to renovate. For the rest of June and part of July, as the restoration of the house continued under Carolyn's demanding eye, he'd been amused and then even impressed by the way David Reid had challenged her and then won her heart.

Love was a funny thing, he mused. Carolyn and he had dated for nearly a year and become good friends but they had never fallen in love. They should have. They each had a demanding profession and a good understanding and tolerance of the demands of each other's jobs. They would have been perfect mates.

For just a moment, the memory of a heart-shaped face, laughing brown eyes and taffy curls slid unasked for into his consciousness. For just a little while last spring, he thought he might have met his soul mate but nothing came of it. Cindy had obviously lost interest and he'd decided that love happened to only a fortunate few.

Putting up the window, Dan got out of the SUV and headed up the hill. He was lucky that Gina, his date, was his receptionist, not only because she was so good at her job but also because she understood when he had to back out of a date at the last minute or in the case tonight, get someone else to pick her up and take her to the party.

He paused for a moment to watch a falling star but didn't make a wish. Instead, he wondered where he was headed with Gina. He'd made no promises, no commitment. He realized he'd just floated along, content to go for coffee with her after a tennis game, to take her out for the odd dinner when she'd stayed late at work and occasionally squire her to a tennis club dinner. He enjoyed her company but . . . He tore his mind away from the direction his thoughts were taking him.

As he neared the lovely Victorian farmhouse, a door opened. A shaft of light spilled over the snow and the sound of voices and laughter reached him. Then the tall figure of a woman appeared and called, "Is that you, Dan? Hurry up. You're missing all the fun."

Carolyn Reid studied Dan as she took his coat from him. He'd always been good-looking; fair-haired, with a whimsical smile and hazel eyes that sparkled when he teased. But tonight she could see he was exhausted. Lines of fatigue spread over his normally cheerful features.

Because Carolyn had been so busy working on the house and trying to get ready for her October wedding, she'd had little time to get together with Dan. David and she had really tried to keep in contact when they returned from their honeymoon but between Dan's heavy workload and their renovations, their meetings had been few and far between.

"Have you had any supper?" she asked.

Dan shook his head. "I was lucky just to get here. The Davidsons' foal kept me out there until an hour ago."

"Then head for the kitchen. I've hired caterers. Just didn't have time to do anything else. Get someone to fix you a plate. I warned them that the odd guest might need more than finger food."

Before heading to the kitchen, Dan poked his head around a doorway that led to the living room and whistled. "You really are putting on the dog. A waitress with a tray! And in the living room, no less," he teased. "Too posh for words."

"You know very well we keep the other wing for family and very close friends. This event is far too grand for the kitchen." Carolyn stuck out her foot to reveal a very pretty shoe. "See, I even left my work boots out back." She gave him a gentle shove and said, "Now, get yourself off to the kitchen and tell the person in charge that you haven't had supper."

With a look of satisfaction, Carolyn watched Dan disappear through the doorway. A voice whispered in her ear, "Ah, dear wife. What are you looking so pleased about?"

Glancing over her shoulder at David, her tall, sandy-haired husband, Carolyn grinned. "I just sent Dan off to the kitchen to ask the caterer for some supper."

"What you are really doing is trying to play Cupid. Admit it."

Carolyn nodded. "Sure I am. I think everyone should be as lucky as we are. And I think our beautiful young caterer is absolutely perfect for Dan. I always did wonder what happened between them last summer."

"And what about Gina?"

Caroline pursed her lips. "I've always figured that Gina was doing the pursuing. Dan sure doesn't act like he's in love."

"Well, let's hope, Cupid, that your little scheme doesn't blow right up in your face."

Upon stepping into the large open space of the second wing of the house, Dan was immediately aware of the delicious smell of cooking. To his left was the family room with the fire burning merrily in the fireplace. A black and white cat rested before it with paws tucked in and eyes closed. To his right, he could see the long harvest table covered with plates of food. A good-looking young man in a white shirt and black pants finished placing some food on a plate, picked it up with a flourish and walked past him just as a young woman slipped into the kitchen and headed for the table to refill her tray. Dan's stomach rumbled in complaint at the aromas wafting by.

The circular kitchen was in the center of the wing. Because the upper cupboards were suspended from the ceiling, he could see part of the figure of a woman working at a counter. Just as he was about to walk over to plead for a meal, the woman stepped out of the kitchen toward the table, holding a pot and tongs and began to place small delicacies on a plate.

Dan froze on the spot. It was Cindy Howard. She turned and saw him, then stilled, the pot in one hand, the tongs in the other. She hadn't changed. She still had a head full of taffy curls and the same heart-shaped face, now flushed from cooking.

For a moment neither of them moved. When a

young serving woman passed between them, it was as if they were both released. As he watched, Cindy seemed to straighten and her chin went up. Then putting down her utensils, she moved toward him, her hand held out. "Hello, Dan," she said coolly. "I understood you were so overworked these days that you'd probably be too busy to come."

The smile she had pasted on her face was not the one Dan remembered. There was no dimple on her left cheek, no twinkle in her lovely brown eyes; just haughty disdain or dislike.

Instead of taking her hand, he pretended not to see it and stuffed his hands into his pants' pockets. "What a surprise," he said insincerely, and then was ashamed of his behavior. "I thought you'd still be at college." He didn't dare touch her hand, didn't dare find out if the physical attraction was still there.

Carefully dropping her hand, she said, "We're off until after Christmas. The course starts again the second week of January." And then, before he could ask anything else, she turned back toward the kitchen and disappeared among the cupboards. He could hear her moving plates and cutlery.

She called out, "Carolyn suggested I should have something substantial on hand in case a guest hasn't had supper. I presume that's why you're in here."

He moved into the kitchen area only to be met by Cindy with a tray holding a steaming bowl of soup, a small loaf of bread and a pottery container of butter. With a nod of her head, she indicated the family area in front of the fireplace. "You can take this tray over there and make yourself comfortable. I hope you enjoy the soup."

Before Dan could say another word, the young

waiter returned and called, "Cindy, we need more of your Thai spring rolls."

Making sure that Dan had a firm grip on the tray, she turned to her assistant. "Right away, Warren."

Now why was she looking down her nose at him as if he was some nasty fungus? She was the one who'd withdrawn from their developing relationship last summer. And without a word of explanation.

He looked gloomily at Charlie, the sleeping cat, and wished he'd stayed at home and gone to bed. As he downed his soup, he watched the comings and goings of the two servers, both very young and full of energy. They made him feel like an old man. Heck, he thought, I'm only twenty-nine, not ninety-two.

Just then Carolyn came in and sat down beside him. "How's the soup?"

"Excellent." Then scowling at her he said, "You might have warned me."

Carolyn tried to look innocent. "Warned you? About what?"

"Don't pretend you don't know what I'm talking about. I'm referring to your new chef."

"Cindy?"

Dan rolled his eyes. "Of course, Cindy."

Ignoring this, Carolyn asked, "Have you told Cindy the soup is excellent?"

"And risk frostbite?" When Carolyn raised an eyebrow in surprise, he mumbled, "I seem to be *persona non gratis.*"

Standing, Carolyn reached for his hand. "Come on. There's no point sitting here feeling sorry for yourself. We're going to start a game."

Dan made a face. "Just what I need."

As he followed her out of the kitchen, he couldn't help but admire Carolyn's elegance. Tonight, she had tied her long dark hair back with a deep crimson bow. She looked very Victorian, with her beautifully embroidered high-necked white blouse and long crimson taffeta skirt. She'd been clever, he thought, to choose an outfit that reflected the period of the house.

Cindy watched Dan and Carolyn leave the area, then turned to prepare another pitcher of punch. She was furious with herself when she saw that her hands were trembling as she poured in the ingredients. She did not want to be affected by the sight of Dan Hamilton. He was history. He'd dropped her like a hot potato last summer and moved on to his receptionist faster than it took to burn oil. And lovely vivacious Gina was here tonight.

Cindy gave the punch a vicious stir. It showed what an idiot she'd been. She'd thought Dan had begun to care as much for her as she had for him. She'd even let her dreams begin to shift in a new direction that included Dan rather than a career as a chef. For a while, she'd imagined a home in Stewart's Falls and a fine tea room or restaurant somewhere in the vicinity.

Well, that was then and this was now. Straightening her back, she picked up the pitcher and headed through the hall toward the living room.

Carolyn had Christmas decorations everywhere. Scented swags of cedar draped the doorways and looped about the beautiful staircase leading to the second floor. A Christmas tree was tucked into the curve of the stairs. Tiny lights reflected off colorful glass balls.

A hubbub of voices greeted Cindy. The game had begun. Some of the guests moved into the hall asking questions and trying to peer over their shoulders to see their backs. In the dining room, she could see others following their example.

David came up to her, dressed in a classy white, collarless shirt and dark trousers, his wild curls tamed and trimmed. "Help me, Cindy. Look at the name on my back. Now, tell me, am I tall or short?"

Cindy read the name 'Napoleon' and grinned. Looking up at her very tall friend, she said, "Very short."

"Ah-h," said David. "Am I one of the seven dwarfs?"

Slipping past him, Cindy called over her shoulder, "Sorry. Wrong guess."

Wending her way through the other guests as they showed their backs to each other, Cindy made it to the dining room with its cherry wood walls and elegant chandelier. Efficiently, she refilled the punch bowl, checked the various plates of food and picked up an empty one, then paused to watch the game in progress. She had to smile while she watched Carolyn's incorrigible brother Ben tease his girlfriend Barbie, giving her outrageous clues. Even Carolyn's quiet brother Andy was nodding as a woman Cindy didn't know asked questions.

She was about to return to the kitchen when she saw Gina, gorgeous in a short red party dress, doing a cutesy little turn to see her back while Dan laughed. Automatically, Cindy shifted her chin a little higher and cut past him without a glance. She sure didn't need to watch Gina rolling her big black eyes and tossing her dark curls.

For a while, Cindy busied herself filling the empty plate. She wished she'd chosen to wear the short black silk dress she occasionally served in. After all, she had legs every bit as good as Gina's. Then she realized what she was thinking and was furious with herself.

Mary Leask

Dan could drool over a dozen brunettes in bright red dresses for all she cared. There were lots of interesting men . . . she corrected herself . . . people to meet. Picking up the plate, she headed back into the dining room.

The game was almost over. Ben and Carolyn were still unable to guess their identities. Instead of helping, the other guests stood around laughing as sister and brother tried to answer the questions honestly while misleading each other. Cindy worked her way into the dining room just as Ben guessed the right answer.

With the game over, old friends hurried into the dining room to say hello and to tell her how great the food was. The art teacher at the high school, Henry Olsen, asked, "When did you take up catering?"

Cindy explained, "My two friends and I decided we might as well use our skills and make a little money so we started doing small jobs. We also used the opportunity to test out our own ideas. Glad you like the food, Henry."

"But how did Carolyn know about this business? She's been so busy we hardly see her anymore."

Carolyn spoke up. "I ran into Cindy in Toronto. We decided to have coffee. When she said she was catering, I hired her immediately."

Dan, standing in the doorway, listened to Cindy as she fielded questions. When she was finished, she turned to head for the kitchen. Dan made as if to speak to her but Cindy ignored him and slipped away.

Watching, David observed the exchange. To his surprise he saw that Dan looked upset. Maybe Carolyn was right. Maybe Dan was carrying a torch for Cindy. He'd been so busy falling in love with Carolyn the previous summer that he hadn't paid much attention when Cindy had stopped seeing so much of Dan. He'd just figured they hadn't hit it off in the end. Anyway,

Gina had been around a lot lately and seemed to have taken over. David was so content himself that it bothered him to see that Dan was unhappy. Even as a little voice warned, *don't interfere*, he wondered what he could do to help them get together again.

Cindy was still fussing with the food, rearranging plates and answering questions when Carolyn touched her arm and said, "Let Warren and Susan look after everything. Come on in and spend part of the evening with the rest of us."

Against her will, Cindy found herself joining a group of people before the tall Christmas tree that sat between two windows in the large rectangular room. Carolyn introduced her to an older couple whose house Carolyn had renovated and another short plump young woman who turned out to be the new librarian. Carolyn's father was there. Cindy was delighted to see how well he looked after having had bypass surgery the previous summer.

Just then, Andy, Carolyn's older brother, played a soft, drawn-out arpeggio on his guitar, announcing he was ready to entertain. Everyone found a place to sit where they could see him. Cindy settled on a cushion beside David and Carolyn before the fireplace.

Andy started with a plaintive old ballad. *"He's gone away for to stay a little while, and he's coming back, though he go ten thousand miles."* The sadness of the song touched Cindy, especially when he sang *"and who will kiss my ruby lips when he's away?"* In spite of herself, she glanced at Dan only to find that he was watching her. Blinking back sudden tears, she hastily looked down.

Dan couldn't help but watch Cindy. When she looked down the sweet line of her neck glowed in the soft light. Andy's ballad brought back all the loneliness and pain he'd felt last summer. She looked up and caught him watching her. Just as suddenly, she looked away again.

A hand touched his arm and Dan found himself looking into Gina's dark eyes. They glowed with an expression he couldn't quite identify. Then, still angry at Cindy, he put an arm around Gina's shoulder. "Sad song," he whispered.

Glancing over at Cindy, he caught her expression. She didn't approve. Tough, he thought, but he didn't feel any better. He hated the way he was acting and the way he'd used Gina to get even with Cindy. With a sigh, he removed his hand from her shoulder and turned to Henry Olsen, who was seated beside him.

When Warren came in and quietly said she was needed, Cindy escaped to the kitchen. She decided to stay there rather than return to the living room. She was too confused by Dan's presence, by the erratic way she was behaving when he was around and by the resentment she felt when she'd seen him at first. It was more than that, she realized. She felt she'd been dealt with unjustly.

With the help of her two servers, Cindy had most of the clean-up done before the guests began to head for home. At Carolyn's insistence, Cindy returned to the hall to say good-night to her friends. It was only as people were heading out that she overheard Gina say to Dan, "Where'd you leave the SUV?"

After their guests had left, Carolyn and David relaxed on the sofa before the fire in the family room. They had already shown Cindy to the newly decorated guest room where she would spend the night. Carolyn was stretched out with her feet on David's lap, smiling blissfully as he worked out the cramps. "Your feet wouldn't hurt so much if you wore those shoes occasionally," he teased. "I'm surprised you didn't figure out a legitimate reason to wear a pair of decorated work boots."

Carolyn grinned. "I was playing chatelaine tonight. Chatelaines wear beautiful shoes."

They relaxed, each thinking their own thoughts. Finally David said, "Well, your efforts at playing Cupid didn't seem to work out. The last I saw of Dan, he was taking Gina home."

Carolyn looked thoughtfully into the fire. "I think Cindy and Dan must have had some kind of misunderstanding. I've known Dan for a long time and I could have sworn he was really very interested in her last summer. I still don't know how Gina got into the act. Dan has never mentioned her when we've had a chance to talk. At least tonight, Cindy and Dan were in the same room. That's a lot better than one of them being in Stewart's Falls and the other in Toronto."

David gave her feet one final pat. "I'm not sure whether that was any advantage or not tonight. Cindy wasn't exactly thrilled to see him."

Wiggling her toes, Carolyn said, "Well, we'll just have to see how we can help them."

"You mean play Cupid?"

"Yup."

"You think that's wise?"

With the look of a dedicated Cupid, Carolyn said, "I think it's their only chance. They need us."

Laughing at that, David eased himself out from under his wife's feet and walked over to the nearby woodpile for more logs. As he placed the logs in the fireplace and closed the door, he said, "I have an idea. I'll take Charlie in to Dan's for his checkup and shots.

I'll see if I can find out anything." When his wife looked skeptical, he added, "We'll talk man to man."

Carolyn laughed. "That ought to do it." Yawning, she stood. "It's bedtime." Nudging the cat with her toe, she said, "Come on, Charlie, we're off."

Stretching carefully, the black and white cat with the white muzzle and black handlebar mustache meowed a few times, then led them up the stairs.

Chapter Two

Dan had short clinic hours on Sundays. He'd tried once canceling Sunday hours in the hope of getting some time to himself. That hadn't worked. People constantly claimed they had emergencies or had to work and couldn't see him any other time. In the end, it had been easier to regulate the time they came.

Entering the examining room, he was surprised to find David trying to convince a reluctant Charlie that it was a good idea to get out of his carrier. Of course, Charlie had more sense. This wasn't the first time he'd been to the vet. And at least one of his visits had been quite unpleasant.

Dan laughed. "Charlie's too smart to let you convince him it's safe to come out of his cage. He's got a good memory. Here, let me."

Unceremoniously he tilted the carrier and a disgruntled Charlie slipped out. Dan caught him as he headed off the examining table. As he stroked the cat

15

for a few minutes to calm him, he said, "That was a very nice party last night. I must say you and Carolyn have done wonders to the house."

"You mean Carolyn has," David corrected, "with the help of her horde of assistants. I'm only useful for holding ladders and tearing out wallboard." They both grinned at that. "Unfortunately," David continued, "Carolyn found out I was also able to use a paintbrush and roller. I finally had to think up a really interesting math problem and escape to my study to work on it."

Dan began to check Charlie over, examining his eyes, ears, mouth and organs. Charlie seemed very healthy. As Dan headed over to a counter to get one of the annual injections for the cat, David said, "Were you surprised to see Cindy?"

Dan busied himself for a moment, carefully administering the rabies shot. Charlie didn't even wince. Finally, Dan answered. "Of course. I thought she'd left Stewart's Falls for good. She certainly cleared out of here in a hurry last August. She didn't even say goodbye."

David was surprised by Dan's bitter tone. For a moment, he hemmed and hawed, then finally decided to take the plunge. "I didn't know that. I thought you two had decided you weren't interested in each other."

Dan had his back to David preparing another injection. "Not so. I thought I'd discovered the woman of my dreams. Just when I was getting ready to pop the question, she dropped me like the proverbial hot potato."

As if he wished he hadn't said so much, Dan briskly gave Charlie his final shot and said, "There you are, Charlie. Good for another year."

He let go of the cat and they both chuckled as Charlie rushed back into the carrier. As Dan fastened the carrier door, he said, "Try to keep him in, David. There's been a lot of snow this year and the odd coyote has been picking up small pets, especially at night."

Thinking of Charlie and the way he had commandeered a spot at the foot of their bed, David said, "I don't think you have to worry about Charlie at night. Since we have heat throughout the house once more, he's decided that he prefers to stay inside."

As David was about to leave the examining room, he remembered the other reason he'd come to see Dan. "By the way, I want to get a puppy for Carolyn for Christmas. Would you have any suggestions? Do you know of anyone that needs a home for a pup?"

Dan thought about it for a moment. "None of my clients' dogs have litters right now; however, I'll phone around. Maybe I can find one that's suitable. Do you want a small or a large dog?"

"I think large rather than small. I'd prefer an intelligent breed rather than one wired only to do one thing. I should have mentioned this earlier but the idea only came to me the other day."

As David bundled an indignant Charlie back into the car, he mumbled to the cat, "Wait until Carolyn hears this. Cindy dumped Dan."

Carolyn sat at the table sipping some of Cindy's wonderful coffee. "How do you manage to make such great coffee? Mine never has much flavor."

Cindy shrugged. "There's nothing to it. I'll show you what I do before I go back to school."

Taking one of the cinnamon buns Cindy had insisted on making, Carolyn nibbled on the icing. Watching Cindy carefully, she said, "You're going to make some guy a great wife. He'll have to run several miles a day to keep in shape if you feed him like you've fed us."

Cindy didn't say anything but she couldn't hide the wistful look that crossed her face.

Carolyn couldn't resist asking, "Cindy, what happened between Dan and you? I thought the two of you would have been engaged by now."

Cindy's stricken expression made her wish she'd minded her own business. Hurriedly, Carolyn said, "I'm sorry, Cindy. I shouldn't have asked. It's none of my business."

Ignoring the apology, Cindy said, "I don't know what happened." She took a bite out of her cinnamon bun and a sip of coffee, then said, "I don't know if you remember that I was to go with Dan to a cousin's wedding. About three days before the wedding, my grandmother in Halifax had a serious heart attack."

Cindy paused and took another bite of the bun. "Gran is special. So the entire family, my mom, dad, and brother and his wife and kids headed out to the east coast to see her. It's easily a two-day trip, but our two cars with alternate drivers made it in thirty-six hours. We were all able to visit with her but within a week she had a massive heart attack and died."

Carolyn said, "I remember, now, that she died. I was very sorry to hear about it. I met your grandmother several times when we did renovations on your parents' house. I really liked her."

"Well," continued Cindy, "I was no sooner back in Ontario and working my first day at the marina when Gina showed up, just at the end of the luncheon period. She struck up a conversation immediately. She began to the describe the wedding that I was to have gone to with Dan. She went to great lengths to let me know the color of the bridesmaids' dresses and added that she'd caught the bouquet. I wasn't exactly thrilled to hear she'd gone with Dan but on the other hand, I was glad he'd had company that day.

"However, then Gina began to mention all the things they'd done while I was away. She was wearing a pretty pair of handcrafted earrings. She made it clear that Dan had purchased them for her at a craft show they'd visited together on the way back from the wedding. Then, just as she left, she said she and Dan were going to Ottawa.

"By then I had received the message loud and clear. Gina was in and I was out. I was so mad, I just packed up and left for Toronto. I was going back to college shortly anyway. A day or so early didn't really matter."

Carolyn's mouth fell open. "Where was I all this time?"

Cindy smiled. "Off on a rosy cloud working like a fiend to make the house livable and to prepare for your wedding."

Carolyn shook her head. "There's something not right here. This doesn't sound like the Dan I know. Are you sure Gina was telling the truth?"

"It certainly sounded like the truth. And anyway, Dan was always saying what a great receptionist she was and how lucky he was to have her. Maybe he decided it would pay to have her in the family," she added cynically.

Carolyn helped herself to another bun and changed the subject. "I know you came up to house-sit your parents' home. Won't you get lonely out at the lake without something to do?"

"Oh, I've got lots to do. We have a major project to hand in before the end of the term. It has to be innovative and practical at the same time."

Carolyn remembered her own days at university when she began to train as an architect. She remembered the effort it took to be innovative and practical at the same time. "Have you any idea what you intend to work on?"

Carolyn was relieved to see that Cindy brightened at this. "Actually, I do and you're responsible for it. You see, the few times my friends, Warren and Susan, and I have catered this past few months, we've had only small jobs and could afford the time and expense to make really exotic hors d'oeuvres. For your party, we needed far more food and had much less time to produce it, so I had to simplify what we were serving. The recipes were mine so I began to think that varying them from complicated to simple while still using at least one major ingredient might be interesting. I might even present the project as a cookbook."

Carolyn was impressed. Cindy's offerings at the party had been quite unique as well as delicious. It was hard to imagine that they could have been better. "Well," she said, "I think the idea is terrific. Feel free to try any of your recipes on us."

Standing and taking her plate and mug to the dishwasher, Cindy said, "I'd better get out to the lake and open the house up. I want to start to work right away."

Going over to Carolyn, she gave her a hug. "Thanks Carolyn, for letting us cater. It was good experience and the money was welcome. And thanks for giving me an excuse to come home. I've been avoiding Stewart's Falls ever since late August.

"One other thing. I'm sure you and David have no secrets from each other. However, I wish you'd tell David a bare minimum about this business with Gina."

*   *   *

David whistled while he rubbed garlic into two steaks. Out of the corner of his eye, he watched his wife chopping lettuce for a salad. He had to smile. She was just as much a perfectionist about making salad as she was working with wood.

He took a moment to admire his heart's desire. Gone was the elegant blouse and long skirt of the night before. Instead, she wore a soft blue shirt and a pair of jeans that showed off her delightfully long legs. However, he had better things to do than admire his wife's legs. He'd been waiting for exactly the right time to tell her what Dan had said. Now, as they were concentrating on preparing supper, seemed the moment to spring his news. Just as he opened his mouth to speak, she asked, "How was Charlie's trip to the vet?"

David laughed. "He was a real coward when it came to getting out of the carrier. Dan had to dump him out on the table. And you should have seen how quickly he got back in when Dan was finished."

Carolyn chopped for another moment, then asked, "How was Dan today?"

David put the steaks on the grill and came over to stand beside Carolyn. "What you really want to know is if I discovered why your efforts at playing Cupid failed."

Putting the lettuce in a bowl, Carolyn turned and said, "Well?"

David hummed and went back to check his steaks.

"Da-vid. You know something. C'mon. Tell me."

David waited a moment for dramatic effect, then said, "Cindy dumped Dan."

He had to laugh at his wife's face. It was obviously the last thing she'd expected him to say.

"She what?"

"Dumped him. Headed back to the big city."

Carolyn shook her head in disbelief. "And who told you that tale?"

"Dan."

"Dan?"

Looking around, David said, "Is there an echo in here?"

"Stop fooling around, David. This is serious. And the steaks are burning."

Returning to the steaks, David turned them over then said, "I'm not fooling. Dan told me all about it."

Carolyn added tomatoes to her salad and took it to the table, removed plates from the heating oven and placed them on a tray, then just stood there, a puzzled look on her face.

When Carolyn didn't respond to his news, David said, "Well? Haven't you anything to say about that?"

Taking baked potatoes from the microwave and placing them on the plates, she said, "There's something very fishy going on here."

Looking at the meat he was cooking, he quipped, "Funny, I thought I was cooking steaks."

"Be serious, David. Something's not right. Cindy told me that Dan dumped her for Gina."

About to put a steak on a plate, David nearly dropped it. "When did she tell you this?"

"This morning while you were out at Dan's with Charlie."

"Well, what do you know."

Carrying their food to the table, they sat down. Carolyn said, "I think it's time we helped straighten things out between them."

David groaned.

Cindy put down her pen and stretched. She'd been slaving over her project for two days without a break and it just wasn't working. It was the organization that was holding her up, not the cooking part of it. There were just too many options. To make matters worse, she'd had to work hard not to think about Dan. Over the two days, her sense that Dan had treated her badly had gathered momentum. However, she thought with determination, she wasn't going to let that interfere.

Straightening her papers and standing, she decided she would go to town and wander through the grocery store. Granted it wasn't as large as those stores found in nearby Smithboro or Toronto. But her project shouldn't depend on ingredients that were hard to get. The health food store also had excellent products. Maybe she'd get an inspiration there.

Getting up, she went over to the dining-room window and looked out. Much to her surprise, she found the wind was bending the pines and driving snow in swirls across the yard. She could hardly see the lake.

Well, that wasn't too clever, she thought with disgust. I should have checked the weather channel or the radio for the forecast.

Then, the wind eased off and it was a little clearer. Now she could see the lake clearly. Looking at her watch, she saw that it was only four o'clock. The grocery store stayed open until six. Surely she'd have time to get into Stewart's Falls and back before dark.

Cindy drove carefully out the back road in her small car. By the time she reached the county road, the snow had intensified again. It was hard to see the cars either in front or behind. Here and there, the wind was blowing long fingers of snow across the road, forcing her to slow down.

Then to make things worse, a van with its headlights on high came up behind her and stayed there. Its nearness made her nervous and when it suddenly roared past her disappearing into a cloud of snow, she was relieved. The snow settled down again and she could dimly see the van ahead of her. Suddenly, its brake lights flared and it wavered toward the center of the road. A second later something flew out of the side of the van.

Cindy didn't have a chance. Before she could get her foot on the brake, she heard a sickening thud and what seemed like a cry of pain. Horrified, she brought her car to a stop at the side of the road and leaped out to check.

The snow was thick again, driving into her face, coating her eyelashes and stinging her cheeks. She began searching along the road, terrified at what she might find. She was sure she'd heard a cry of pain. It had sounded like an animal. Glancing over her shoulder, she looked to see if the van was returning. Surely it would stop and someone would come back to discover who or what had fallen out. But there was nothing to see except streamers of snow sifting over the banks left by the plow.

She was just about to give up when she heard a whimper. She stopped and listened. Again she heard the sound, louder this time. Carefully she eased herself down the bank beside the road toward the sound. Then she saw it. Already partially covered with snowflakes, a puppy lay on its side. The minute it realized she was there it tried to struggle to its feet only to cry out with pain and flop back down.

Cindy couldn't believe it. Someone had thrown a puppy out on the road in front of her car. Speaking softly, she knelt down near the young creature. She remembered that animals in pain or frightened could bite in defense so she sat for a moment and let the little beast see she meant no harm. Finally, she got up the courage to stretch out her gloved hand and let it sniff her. To her relief, it nuzzled into her hand and then broke her heart by crying pitifully. Again it tried to move and she could see that it couldn't put weight on one of its front legs.

Cindy sat back on her heels trying to decide what to do. She couldn't leave it and get help because she was sure she would never find the location again while it snowed so heavily. Finally she made a decision. Going back to her car, she reversed along the shoulder until she was close to the puppy. Opening her trunk, she pulled out the shovel she always carried in the winter. Although not long, it was sturdy and had a wide blade. First she spread a blanket over the trunk, then took the shovel and waded down into the ditch. Standing below the puppy and talking to it all the time, she carefully eased the shovel under it. The puppy yelped once as she began to lift it and then collapsed into a sorry bundle of yellow fur.

Struggling up out of the ditch was not easy but she made it and carefully slid the puppy off the shovel and onto the blanket in the trunk. She paused for a moment and stroked it. She was really concerned now. Its eyes had lost their glow and it seemed to have trouble breathing. She hated to close the trunk on it but it was the only way.

Hopping into the car, she started it and continued toward town just as fast as she dared. When she reached the first street, she turned toward Dan's animal hospital. Not for a moment did she think of her resentment toward Dan. All that she could think of was that he would help the puppy. Of that she was sure.

Cindy could see by the car clock that it was nearly four-thirty when she turned into his parking lot. She tried the clinic door and found it locked. She could have wept. Running around to the back where she knew Dan had an apartment, she pounded on the door.

Dan was just making supper when he heard someone banging on his back door. He sighed. Not another emergency! Shoving the meat he'd just taken out back into the refrigerator, he hurried to see who it was.

Cindy was standing there, snow coating her curls and her jacket. It was what he'd dreamed of happening all day; that she would suddenly come to his door with her happy smile and then everything would be right between them. It took a second for him to realize that Cindy was clearly distressed.

Before he could ask what was wrong, she cried, "I have a wounded puppy. I hit it on the road. Oh please, say you'll see it."

"The puppy's in the car?" he asked briskly. She nodded. "Then I'll get my bag and a board and come to the front and open up the door. Bring the car as close as you can. Don't try to move the puppy. I'll examine it first."

As soon as Cindy had the car by the door and the trunk opened, Dan checked the puppy over. The poor little thing was hardly reacting to his touch. Satisfied that it was possible to move the animal, he said, "Cindy, I want you to help me by slipping this board under the pup when I lift it up. Then, if you'll take one end, I'll take the other and we'll move it into the examining room. He appears to have a broken leg. There may be other injuries so we'll have to be careful."

When the puppy was safely transferred to the examining table, Dan said, "I don't think I can wait while I phone for an assistant. Do you think you could help me?"

"I'll do anything you want."

Dan smiled at her, and she could have sworn her heart levitated. Get a grip, she thought. Concentrate on the puppy.

Dan talked as he worked on the puppy, more to calm Cindy than anything else.

Shining a light into the puppy's eyes, he said, "His pupils are the same size and they're reacting to light. That's a relief." He continued his examination by checking the puppy's mouth. There were no signs of a break or of vomiting.

Giving her a reassuring smile, he said, "I don't think he's suffered any head trauma. But I don't like the way he's breathing."

He ran his hands gently over the puppy's chest. "I'm feeling for any areas that would indicate escaped air under the skin. It would feel crinkly like air under cellophane. It's called 'crepitus'. It may mean there is damage to the puppy's lung, probably caused by a broken rib." He stopped at one place. "And I'm afraid I've found such a spot. When the puppy bounced up against your car's undercarriage, he may have broken some ribs. He probably broke his leg at the same instant since the injury is on the same side."

"Can you fix it?" Cindy asked anxiously.

"When I've finished checking for other injuries, I'll put a pressure pad over the crinkly area and hold it with a wide elastic bandage."

Dan was aware of an unnatural tremor in Cindy's voice and when he looked up at her, he could see that she was visibly trying to control the fact that she was shaking.

Concerned, he said, "Cindy. I haven't eaten since breakfast. I'm dying for a cup of tea. Could you go into my office and fill the electric tea kettle? There's a tea pot there. You'll find tea bags and mugs and anything else you need."

While Cindy made the tea, Dan continued checking the puppy's abdomen and tail for any other injuries.

By the time she returned, he was gently palpating the injured leg to determine the type of break. "I've found a break in the radius and the ulna. With a puppy this young, it should heal with a splint rather than putting on a cast. This will allow the puppy to grow without damaging the circulation which might occur if I used a heavy cast. I'll have to change the splint regularly to accommodate the puppy's growth."

Smiling at Cindy to reassure her, he said, "Will you watch the puppy while I get some sedative, bandages and a splint?" She nodded and proceeded to stroke the puppy's soft yellow head.

He returned with the prepared injection. "Hold the puppy's head firmly while I administer this sedative. It will relieve any pain he's experiencing."

She watched as he carefully injected the drug into the puppy's hind leg. The puppy whimpered. "Thanks for the help, Cindy. Now, while the medication is taking effect, I'll get a blanket and some hot water bottles for you to place around the little guy."

Quickly, Dan returned with the blankets and hot water bottles. Together they made the puppy as comfortable as possible. Then, Dan returned to his office for the needed cup of tea. Unbeknownst to Cindy, he'd laced hers with several spoonfuls of sugar.

Taking the tea from Dan, Cindy sipped it gratefully. Dan laughed when she made a face. "It's good for you. The sugar will make you feel better."

When they had finished, Dan said, "It looks like the puppy is relaxed enough for me to take an X-ray." Going across the room, he picked up two heavy lead aprons. "I want you to put on one of these protective coverings and protective gloves so that you can hold him steady while I take pictures of his bad leg and his chest."

He watched Cindy carefully as she followed his instructions. She was pale and her hands still trembled. As he wheeled over the portable X-ray, he asked, "How did this happen? I can't imagine what a puppy this age was doing out in a storm at this time in the evening."

"He wasn't. Someone deliberately threw him out of a van right in front of me."

"You're sure?"

"Positive. A van came right up behind and tailgated me for maybe half a mile and then roared past me and disappeared into a terrific cloud of snow. Just when I thought I'd seen the last of it, the snow cleared and there it was right in front of me. Suddenly, it veered toward the center and at the same moment, I could see something fall out of the side of it. A second later, I felt a thump and heard a cry." Cindy's eyes filled with tears. "I didn't have a chance, Dan. I hit him."

For a moment, Dan forgot his anger and hurt. He could have banged his head against the X-ray machine. Here was Cindy needing to be held and comforted, and he was on the other side of the examining table with his hands full of injured puppy. "Cindy. You did the very best you could. You used your head and brought him in without adding to his injuries."

She gave him a watery smile and something inside him somersaulted. And then he remembered how she'd left him without a word of explanation and hardened his heart. He'd been there, done that.

When Dan finished taking and developing the films, he brought them in to show Cindy. Pointing at them, he said, "Look, you can see that a rib is broken and that the breaks in the leg are clean."

Stroking the small animal's blond head, he continued, "I'll insert an intravenous line so that I can medicate him to protect him from shock and infection. Then I'll wrap the chest to help seal the air leak and stabilize the broken rib and finally, I'll set the leg."

Dan thought, as he lifted the sedated puppy off of the examining table and carried him to a waiting cage, that Cindy could not have done better. She'd followed his instructions calmly and efficiently as he'd set the pup's broken leg.

She opened the door and watched anxiously while Dan placed the puppy gently on the blankets and hot water bottles she'd placed in the cage. Unable to stop herself, she reached in and stroked the small animal's fur.

"He'll be fine," Dan assured her. "Come on into the apartment and relax for a moment." Then, in spite of himself, he put his arm across her shoulders and led her toward the back of the building.

Cindy actually leaned against him. He could see that she was exhausted. Then, as if suddenly realizing where she was, she straightened up. So much for that, David thought wryly, as she preceded him through the door to his very large kitchen.

Going to the refrigerator, he began to hunt for something to offer her to eat. As he searched through its contents, he watched Cindy out of the corner of his eye. Instead of collapsing in a kitchen chair, she was moving restlessly around, looking at a veterinarian's journal he'd left on the table, peeking out a window into the darkness and examining a colorful calendar sent out annually by the maker of a popular pet food.

Hoping to ease her tension, he asked, "What were you doing out in that snow storm? I thought you were staying with Carolyn and David."

"I stayed with them last night. I'm staying at my parents' place for the rest of the holidays. They really like it when someone is there while they're away in Florida. They often let friends stay for free just to have the place lived in. Anyway, I have to work out recipes for my major project. My mother's kitchen is better-equipped than the one in the house I share with three other students so I decided to do the work up here."

Dan tried to ignore the little skitter of hope that lifted his heart. If she was staying around, at least he'd be able to discover what had gone wrong.

Dan peered out the window at the storm. "Does that mean that you're planning to go back out to the lake now?"

Cindy looked surprised at that question. "Of course."

"Well, there's no way you'd make it back on that road tonight. It'll be blown right in."

Ruffled by this high-handed announcement, she said, "Well, I'm not planning to stay here."

Now why was she so angry? he thought to himself. Then he realized what she had just said. Closing the fridge door, he said grimly, "I didn't ask you to, Cindy."

Fascinated, he watched her blush. Then she gave him a glittery look that could have frozen water. "I didn't suppose you had."

Frustrated, Dan got up and headed to the telephone. First he called Peter, a high-school student who worked part-time cleaning up at the clinic. He was only too happy to come over and stay with the puppy. Then he called David and Carolyn. Ignoring Cindy's indignant glare, he explained what had happened and asked if he could bring Cindy over for the night.

Turning to Cindy, he said, "It's all arranged. Peter said he wouldn't mind some overtime. He's going to come in and stay with the puppy for the evening. Carolyn said they'd already eaten but that we should both come and have some of that delicious soup you made yesterday. I'll drive us to their place and one of them can bring you back in the morning."

Dan could tell from the mulish look on her face that she didn't like him taking over but there was no way he was going to let her go off in that storm down that twisting road to the lake. "Come on, let's go and check on the puppy. Peter only lives up the road. He'll be here in a moment."

The thought of the puppy made Cindy forget Dan's highhandedness for the moment and she hurried back to check on him.

It was all Dan could do not to hum out loud. It did not matter that he could barely see beyond the front of the car. Nor did it matter that Cindy was sitting beside him like a small ruffled bird or that waves of indignation were vibrating around the car's interior. Now that he'd had time to think about the situation, he'd decided that things weren't as bad as they seemed. After all, Cindy had come to him when she needed help. At least it meant she still had some regard for him.

Where else would she go? a little voice asked. *You're the only vet in town.* He ignored the voice. Instead, he had to plan. There was no way he was going to let Cindy write him off before he found out exactly why she'd dropped him last summer. He had to know or he'd never be able to get on with his life.

He wanted a wife, a home and a family. If she didn't want him, then he had to know why.

David opened the door for them and was met with a flurry of snow as they entered. As Cindy handed him her jacket and stepped out of her snow boots, she apologized, "I'm sorry to dump myself on you again, David. I'm sure I could have made it home. Dan was just being a tin pot dictator."

As they headed into the family wing with its open kitchen, dining room and family room, Carolyn met them and asked, "What's this about a puppy with a broken leg?"

Before Dan could answer, Cindy said, "Someone threw a puppy out of their van right in front of my car. I couldn't help but hit it. But Dan has been wonderful. He checked the puppy over and set the leg."

Dan rolled his eyes at David and muttered, "First I'm a dictator. Now I'm a hero."

Carolyn had the table set for the two of them and quickly ladled out the soup. There was also a basket of rolls and a plate of leftover hors d'oeuvres from the night before. Dan and Cindy quickly availed themselves of both.

Carolyn wondered out loud, "Could those people have dropped any more puppies out of their van?"

Dan thought about it for a moment. "I suppose it's possible. They might have tried to get rid of an entire litter."

"How old is the puppy and what kind?" asked David.

Between sips of soup, Dan said, "Somewhere between nine and twelve weeks, I'd think. Certainly no older. It's a good-looking puppy. Mostly if not all golden retriever. But there's no registration on the puppy's ear."

Dan could see that Cindy was upset by the idea of more puppies. She turned to him. "You don't suppose there are more out in this storm?"

"I hope not."

Carolyn brought coffee and a plate of cookies and squares to the table. "They could have dropped more puppies in town in the hopes that they'd be picked up. It's a perfect night to get away with such a thing."

For a while, Cindy and Dan concentrated on eating. Carolyn poured coffee for herself and David. As she sipped her coffee, she began to twist a loose tendril of hair. Recognizing the habit, David wondered just what was going on in her head.

Suddenly Carolyn looked up and said, "Did you know that the Health Center had an open house for their patients last week? It was really great. They had all kinds of delicious goodies."

Where is she going with this? David wondered and then noticed that Carolyn was looking right at Dan. Suddenly, David caught on. He had to stifle a laugh. He knew the minute Dan made the connection. However Dan proceeded to finish off his cookies without saying anything.

David leaned back to check that his wife hadn't sprouted wings.

"What on earth are you doing?" Carolyn whispered.

"I'm checking to see if you have grown wings," he whispered back.

For a second, Cindy looked at them, interested in the whispers and then continued eating. When she was finished digging into the cookies and squares and sipping coffee, Dan made his move.

"I've been sitting here thinking about the Medical Center having a spread for their clients. I'd like to do something like that just before Christmas. I could kill two birds with one stone. I'm hoping to have a new associate by that time so I could not only have open house but also have people meet the new vet."

This was news to them all. "You've actually got someone in mind?" asked Carolyn.

"I'm interviewing an experienced veterinarian to-morrow. This person is anxious to move up to this area. She comes highly recommended and has an extra qualification in skin diseases. I'm just keeping my fingers crossed. I'm really desperate for help."

Never one to let an opportunity slip by, Carolyn said, "I think the notion of an open house is a great idea. When would you do it?"

Dan thought for a moment, then said, "Probably the Saturday before Christmas. That's if Cindy's available."

Cindy nearly dropped her coffee. "Me? What have I to do with it?"

"I hoped I could hire you to cater. Also, I think you'd probably have to have some assistance. Maybe one of the people who came up to serve at your party. What do you think?"

All three of them held their breath while Cindy mulled over the suggestion. They breathed a collective sigh of relief when Cindy said, "It wouldn't be cheap."

Dan smiled at Cindy. "I want the best." She blushed.

The Cupids present kicked each other under the table.

When they finished their coffee, Dan went to the window to check on the weather. The snow was blowing sideways. The yard lights were barely visible. David looked over Dan's shoulder. "Why don't you stay tonight. We've lots of room. First thing tomorrow, I'll plow out our lane. I imagine the county road will be clear by then."

From the other side of the room, Carolyn piped up, "That's a good idea." David marveled at the excellence of Cupid ears.

Dan shook his head. "Someone needs to be there to check the puppy."

"Couldn't Peter?" asked Cindy. "Didn't you say he wanted some extra overtime?"

Dan turned to find Cindy right behind him. She had a gratifyingly anxious look in her eyes when she said, "I think it's too stormy for you to drive."

As Cindy and the two Cupids watched, Dan went over to the telephone and called Peter. When he was assured by Peter that the puppy was fine and the three cats being boarded were just dandy, and that he would be glad to stay the night, Dan agreed to stay over.

"Great," said David. "We can have a game of Scrabble."

Carolyn rolled her eyes. "He loves Scrabble but," glancing at Dan who was swallowing a yawn and Cindy, who had dark shadows under her eyes, "I think we should save the game for another night. It's ten o'clock and with Dan's luck, he could still be called out. Anyway, he's almost asleep on his feet. And Cindy's exhausted."

Cindy couldn't argue with that but she had an idea. "Why don't we have a game out at my parents' place some evening? I'll cook us up something delicious. You bring the Scrabble game."

David and Caroline couldn't agree fast enough.

Trying to glance at Dan casually, Cindy said, "Would you be free to come, Dan?"

The Cupids held their breath.

"I'd love to," Dan said. "I just have one problem."

The Cupids' shoulders drooped with disappointment.

"I'll have to see what evening I can line up with Fred Somers up at Cobi Lake. He usually covers me one night a week. How about next Tuesday as a possibility?"

Dan was gratified to see Cindy's face light up at this. "Tuesday's fine with me," she said. "I'd like an opportunity to serve all three of you to show my appreciation for all you've done for me."

Tuesday was perfect with everyone.

Getting up, Carolyn said, "Come upstairs. I'll show you to your rooms. Cindy, you can have the room you had before. I haven't changed the bedding yet. I'll lend you a sleep shirt. It shouldn't be too long for you." Turning to Dan, she said, "I'm afraid you'll have to sleep in one of the rooms that are only dry-walled. We haven't had time to decorate it yet."

Dan couldn't resist saying, "You're sure the ceiling is safe?"

Both Carolyn and David exchanged glances as they remembered the time the old plaster had come down on David's head.

Grinning like mad, Dan continued, "I don't have to wear a yellow shower cap while I'm in there, do I?"

"You watch out," warned David, "or you'll end up in a storage cupboard that has not been renovated. There are spiders and dust and lots of hanging plaster."

"What are you all talking about?" asked Cindy.

"Get Dan to tell you about it sometime. He seemed to think the entire incident was hilarious," replied Carolyn and led the way upstairs.

Chapter Three

When Cindy entered the kitchen the next morning, she discovered it was empty. There was a pot of coffee on the counter with a note from Carolyn saying that she was in her workroom and to come and get her.

Coffee mug in hand, Cindy wandered into Carolyn's workroom only to discover she was working at one of her wonderful models. "You should have wakened me, Carolyn. I could have been out of your hair by now."

Carolyn looked up from what she was doing. "I thought you needed a good rest. Yesterday was pretty stressful, what with the storm and hitting the puppy. Wait just a moment while I glue in this piece and I'll come in and have coffee with you while you eat. I have to go to town after so I'll take you into Dan's to get your car."

Cindy wandered over to peek at Carolyn's model. "What a beautiful house this is going to be. Are you designing it for someone special?"

Carolyn couldn't resist playing Cupid. "The house is for Dan. I'm just working on a few ideas right now. It's going to be built on a lovely lot that extends down into a ravine with a stream that flows into the lake below the falls. The location is perfect for Dan. It's only two minutes' drive back to the animal hospital. I think he hopes the new veterinarian will want to live in his apartment once the house is built."

This house was very different from Carolyn's. It was a long sprawling bungalow. At one end there was a master bedroom and bath. A study was next to it. In the central part of the house was the entrance and the traditional kitchen, family room, dining and living room. The kitchen was fantastic; large with lots of working space and storage. The other end of the house consisted of bedrooms and bathrooms.

Cindy was impressed. "Is there a basement level?"

"Yes," answered Carolyn. "It will be built back into the hill so that you can walk out onto the lawn through double doors. I haven't made a model of it yet. Dan's going to finish it himself later on."

"The house has a fabulous kitchen, Carolyn. It's a chef's dream."

"Dan thought his wife should have a great space to work in. He felt the kitchen was the most important room in the house."

Cindy's heart hit the floor. She could literally feel it bounce. "Dan's marrying Gina? How come you didn't mention that before now?"

Quite pleased by Cindy's reaction, Carolyn paused for a moment before saying, "As far as I know, Dan has never mentioned he's getting married to anyone. He came to me early last August and asked me to develop a plan for a house on the lot he had just bought. He plans to have it built this spring. I think he was just looking forward to the day when he would meet someone and marry. Come on, I'm ready for a break and you need breakfast."

Still rattled by the idea that Dan might be getting married, Cindy followed Carolyn along to the kitchen and sat while Carolyn made her breakfast. Suddenly realizing what she was doing, she sprang to her feet. "What am I thinking of. For goodness sake, I can make my own breakfast."

"You made the cinnamon buns and the soup we had yesterday. Today, it's my turn."

As Cindy worked her way through a serving of very delicious French toast, Carolyn asked, "What kind of things are you going to serve at Dan's open house?"

Cindy thought for a moment. "I'm not sure. I'll have to meet with Dan and find out exactly what he has in mind."

Carolyn couldn't help a smug little grin when she realized that her plan to get them together was working. Then she had another idea. "I think I know of two high-school kids that would make good servers."

"That's a great idea. It would save Dan a little money. I doubt that we'd do anything as elaborate as we did at your place. After all, people are just dropping in. They're not staying for the evening."

As Cindy finished her breakfast, she asked, "When did Dan go back?"

"David was up at seven plowing out our lane. Fortunately, the county road was already clear so Dan was able to get to work by eight o'clock. By the way, he said that you should come in to see the puppy when you go over to get your car."

Carolyn paused for a moment and then asked, "Just how badly was the puppy hurt? I didn't like to ask too much about it for fear it might upset you."

"His front leg and a rib were broken and his lung was punctured. I was really lucky Dan was home. I think the pup would have died otherwise."

"That sounds like a very expensive treatment, Cindy." At the look of panic on Cindy's face, Carolyn tried to change the subject. "Do you really have time in your life for a puppy? For that matter, do you have the space for a puppy where you live in Toronto?"

Cindy brought her hands to her face in dismay. "You know, I didn't think of the expense or what I would do with the pup. I just knew I needed to get help for the puppy and that Dan was the person who could do it. I-I'll have to talk to Dan about paying him so much a month. And I'll have to start searching for a home for the pup. There's no way we could keep him at the place I share with three other students."

Carolyn had asked her questions out of curiosity. She hadn't meant to upset Cindy. On the other hand, she was pretty sure that Dan had been only too glad to help her. "I'm sure you and Dan can work something out."

Cindy stood and took her dishes to the sink. Quickly, she washed the dishes while Carolyn dried them. "I'm going to see Dan as soon as we get there and discuss the costs with him."

When Cindy entered Dan's clinic, she saw Gina at the reception desk. *Oh great,* she thought. However, she marched right up and said, "Hi, Gina. Dan said I could come to see the puppy any time I wanted. I'll just go through."

She could see that Gina didn't like that at all; however, Dan must have spoken to her for she watched silently as Cindy headed through to the cages where the puppy was kept.

The puppy heard her coming and tried to raise himself on his good paw. Opening the cage, Cindy reached in and stroked his head. "How are you, little fellow?" The puppy made a contented sound and butted his head against her hand, then licked her fingers. Today, his eyes were much clearer and the IV had been removed.

Cindy admired his soft golden fur. "You have got to be mostly Golden Retriever with a lovely coat like that." She scratched his ears. "I think you need a name. Let's see." She thought for a moment. "I've got it. We'll call you Crash."

Just then she heard a noise down the hall and looked up to see Dan coming out a door. A short slim redhead followed. Dan swung his arm over her shoulders and made some remark Cindy couldn't catch. The redhead burst into laughter.

Cindy wanted to scratch her eyes out. She was appalled at the swiftness of that thought and then she recognized it for what it was. Sheer, unmitigated jealousy.

At that moment Dan noticed her and called, "Cindy. Come and meet my new associate."

Closing the cage carefully, Cindy turned to meet them as they moved down the hall. Dan said to the woman beside him, "Merry, I'd like you to meet chef extraordinaire, Cindy Howard. She's the person who is going to supply the goodies when you meet our clients."

Turning to Cindy, he said, "Meet our new veterinarian, Dr. Meredith Johnson. 'Merry' for short. She has agreed to move to Stewart's Falls and work with me as soon as possible."

Cindy's heart sank. Meredith was beautiful. She

was petite with bright blue eyes and a lovely complexion. She didn't even have freckles.

Meredith held out her hand and welcomed Cindy with a sweet smile. And I'm not even going to be able to dislike her, Cindy thought as she shook her hand.

"Hi, Cindy. Dan tells me you rescued that lovely puppy and that you helped him set his leg."

Disarmed by the doctor's openness, Cindy could only mumble, "It was the least I could do."

Dan turned to Cindy. "Look, I want to see Merry out. I'll be back in a moment." Then as he passed the puppy's cage, he said, "Our patient looks like he had a good night. We're going to have to think of a name for him."

"Crash," Cindy said.

"Crash?"

"I thought it would make a good name."

Dan grinned. "I think it's perfect. When he starts to move around with that splint on his leg, he's going to be very awkward. He'll earn his name. Wait here. I'll be back in a few minutes."

Cindy petted the puppy again but her mind wasn't on what she was doing. She was still shaken by the force of her jealousy when she'd seen Dan's arm around Merry. She thought she'd buried all her feelings for him.

When Dan reentered the area containing the puppy he couldn't help but notice Cindy's frown. Maybe, he thought, she was worried about the puppy. Walking up to her, he tried to assure her. "Crash is doing very well. He's quite alert in spite of the medication and has no fever. You don't have to worry about him, Cindy."

She surprised him by saying, "Dan, could we sit down and talk somewhere?"

Wondering what she wanted to talk about, he said, "Let's go into my office. We can have coffee and cookies while we talk."

Dan poured coffee into two mugs, added milk to hers and placed it near her on his desk.

Surprised, Cindy said, "You remembered how I like it."

"I haven't forgotten anything about you, Cindy."

What did she make of a remark like that? Did it mean she was special to him or was it that he just had a good memory? Unaware that she was clenching her hands together, she tried to lead into her problem. "You probably never knew that I can be absent-minded."

Dan opened his mouth to object but she continued, now twisting a ring on her finger. "I was so frantic about the puppy that I just marched in here and expected you to treat him. I never thought of the care he would take or what would happen to him after he recovered." She picked up her coffee mug and nervously ran her finger around its rim. "I didn't even ask you about the cost." Looking at him defiantly, she said, "I'm hoping we can work out a payment schedule and that I can help you find him a home."

For a second, Dan was furious. How dare she think he'd charge her. Taken back by the intensity of his reaction, he realized that his feelings for Cindy had not diminished. They were certainly strong enough that he had no intention of letting her pay for the puppy's treatment. The problem was whether he wanted to risk having her reject him again.

He also knew that as a student, Cindy could never save the cost of the puppy's treatment and that pride would make it difficult for her to accept help. Then the perfect solution occurred to him.

"I'll make you a deal, Cindy. You cater my open house and, in exchange, I'll look after Crash. And don't go making fantastic things for the occasion. Just small sandwiches and cakes that people can nibble on while they walk around." Recalling good-looking young Warren who had served at Carolyn and David's, he added, "And forget about getting professional help from Toronto. I know some high-school kids who would be glad to serve for minimum wage."

"That's what Carolyn said," Cindy mumbled.

"Come on, Cindy. Look at me. Is it a deal?"

Finally she looked at him directly. "Okay. I accept. But what are we going to do with Crash?"

"Leave that with me. I have an idea that might just work. I'll have to make some inquiries. I'm finished for the morning and I'm starving. Share a sandwich with me before you go out to the cottage."

What else could she say but yes. Her relief knowing that she was never going to have to pay for the puppy's care was enormous. It was at that moment that she realized that she wasn't going to be able to walk away from Dan without first discovering why he'd dropped her.

Her spirits definitely on the mend, Cindy followed Dan back into the apartment. "Let me make lunch. You've been working all morning." With a devious little smile, she added, "You can tell me all about your beautiful new associate." There was nothing like knowing the competition.

Stepping back from the cupboards, Dan said, "The kitchen is all yours. Just make something fast and simple. I'll set the table and tell you about Meredith."

Cindy listened as she poked around the kitchen. She soon found what looked like homemade barley soup in the freezer and a can of salmon for sandwiches.

Dan talked as he set the table. "Meredith was several years ahead of me at veterinarian college. She was popular with all the younger students; always willing to help us out. She was also a terrible tease. I had no idea that the Dr. Meredith Johnson I was planning to interview was Merry. Her maiden name was Harper. I wasn't aware that she'd married. Even then, I would have expected her to keep her own name. Usually, professional women do. It just keeps the record-keeping clearer."

Dan made coffee as he continued. "It turned out that there were no less than two Meredith Harpers already registered at the College of Veterinarians. It seemed easier to take her husband's name. They joined her husband's father in his practice in a suburb of Toronto."

Cindy couldn't resist asking the obvious question. "Why has she decided to leave that practice?" What she really wanted to know was whether Merry was divorced and available to charm Dan.

Dan was quiet for a moment. Glancing over at him, she saw that his expression was grave. "Two years ago, her husband was killed in an automobile accident while out on an emergency call. Merry tried to keep the practice going but found her heart just wasn't in it. She decided she needed a new beginning."

"What about her husband's father?"

"He had already retired. Her in-laws think she is doing the right thing. They have been very supportive. Merry sold her practice a month ago. She thinks she can be up here before Christmas."

Cindy brought a plate of sandwiches to the table and served up the soup. They talked about nothing in particular for a few minutes before Dan said, "I have just one other problem. If Merry is to come up here, I have to find accommodation for her."

"Will that be difficult?"

"Possibly. You see, Merry has a four-year-old son. Also, she wants a temporary place to stay until she's sure that working up here is what she wants. If we hit it off, then she'll become a partner and she'll buy herself a new home."

"Why don't you ask Carolyn about a house. She seems to know about everything happening in town." But what Cindy was really thinking was that maybe, just maybe she had found a way to show her appreciation to Dan. She would ask her parents if Merry could use her parents' place after she left. That would give Merry time to find a place in town she really liked.

They cleaned up together. Cindy began to relax. It seemed like old times until Dan asked, "How are your plans coming when you finish college. Where do you plan to go to polish your skills? The last time I heard you talk about this, you mentioned Paris or Rome. That was your dream, wasn't it?"

Cindy busied herself for a moment wiping out the sink. Just how was she to mention that her dreams might have changed without being obvious. Finally, she said, "All cooking students start off with plans to become the greatest chefs in the world. By the time we graduate, reality has set in. I think I would be happy to be a chef or caterer anywhere as long as I found it interesting and was able to do my best."

With that, she stepped back from the sink, gave Dan one of her most dazzling smiles and said, "I'd better get off to my parents' place. I have work to do."

"Work?" Dan asked.

"Don't you remember? I have to produce a term

project while I'm up here. I'll just say goodbye to Crash and then head out to the lake. I'm sure the road will be cleared by now."

Dan watched her go, her head high, her taffy curls bouncing as she walked. He frowned at the little niggle of hope he'd felt when she'd said that she could be happy anywhere.

Carolyn put the lid on the small can of paint she was using and cleaned her brush. She walked around her model, checking to see that every detail was correct. Everything was perfect. With a sigh, she looked around her workroom. There was nothing else to do.

She walked through the door into David's study. He had his nose glued to the computer screen, his fingers dancing over the keyboard. Unable to resist, she walked quietly up to him, put her hands on his shoulders, leaned forward and nuzzled his cheek.

David leaned into her cheek and said, "What's up?"

Carolyn sighed again and said, "I shouldn't have decided to put off the renovations at the Pierces' until after Christmas. I feel as if I'm in limbo."

She walked about his study, reading titles of books and straightening pictures. "I'm bored."

"I thought you were working on the model of Dan's home."

"It's finished."

"When?"

"Just now."

David turned and laughed at her. "You haven't had time to be bored. You just wanted an excuse to bother me."

Before Carolyn could give him a poke on the arm, the telephone rang. David answered it and handed it to Carolyn. "It's Phil Bendon. He says he has an emergency. It's urgent he speak to you."

Carolyn made a face. "What emergency?" she mouthed.

David shrugged his shoulders.

"Hi Phil," said Carolyn. "How can I help?" She listened while Phil described what he needed in great detail.

When she hung up, she turned to David. "There's a problem with the Stewart's Falls Santa Claus Parade."

David raised his eyebrows in question.

Rubbing her hands together with glee, Carolyn said, "Santa's sled has bit the dust. I understand the reindeer have gone to reindeer heaven and if we don't come to the rescue, Santa will not make it next Saturday to our illustrious parade."

"We?" said David.

Giving her husband a peck on the cheek, Carolyn said, "Of course, 'we'. I'm counting on you. I'm going to make supper so that we can be over to see the floats by seven."

Carolyn was heading out the study door when she came to a halt. Twisting a tendril of hair by her ear, she said, "David, I've just had an idea."

Oh, oh, David thought. I know the signs. Something's brewing. "Yes, dear," he said meekly.

"Let's see if we can get Dan and Cindy to help. Will you telephone Dan and see if he's free. Suggest he ask Cindy to help, too."

David got up and came over to Carolyn. "No, my sweet. He's your old flame. You telephone him. Anyway, you're the one that knows exactly what's wrong with the floats. And you're the one so keen to play Cupid."

Making a face at him, Carolyn shrugged and said, "Okay."

Cindy sat curled up in front of the fireplace, a writing pad on her lap. Ripping off another sheet with disgust, she threw it on the floor. Looking around ruefully, she decided she'd have enough crumpled pages to start another fire. Glancing at her watch, she saw that it was four o'clock. She'd wasted the entire afternoon trying to make her idea work. It was beginning to look like it had been far too ambitious. Certainly too complicated. To make it worse, she was getting bored, something she never felt when thinking about food.

Just then the telephone rang. To her surprise, it was Dan.

"Are you free?" he asked. "Carolyn has an emergency."

Immediately, Cindy had visions of an accident. "What kind of emergency?"

"She's been called in by the Santa Claus Parade Committee to rescue some of the permanent floats." It was with relief that she heard Dan continue. "They were stored in a less than ideal location and got wet. Just to add to the problem, something fell on them. The combination seems to have spelled disaster. They need to be repaired or replaced by next Saturday. Could you come over to the old warehouse where they're stored right after supper? She thinks it would be best if David, you and I give her hand evaluating the damage. When she knows what she has to do, she'll enlist the tennis club to help repair them."

Cindy couldn't say yes fast enough. It would give her a chance to escape her fruitless work on the project, a chance to help Carolyn and, if she was honest, an opportunity to spend more time with Dan. Maybe if she was back with the summer crowd working on parade material just as they had on the play last June and July, things would sort themselves. At least then, she might be able to understand what had gone wrong and get on with her life.

"I'd love to help her. What time tonight?"

"About seven. If you like, I could pick you up."

Cindy hesitated only for a moment. "That would be great, if you don't mind."

Cindy and Dan arrived at the old warehouse just as Carolyn and David were getting out of their truck. Cindy recognized Phil Bendon, the local pharmacist waiting at the door.

Phil was saying, "You won't believe it, Carolyn. Santa's sled is in shambles. So is the float that was used to hold the carolers. Something fell from the roof on it. I think that summer storm we had back in August must have damaged the roof. Anyway, there's a hole in it now. We're going to move what's left of the floats to a dryer location. That's if you think you can repair or replace them in the next week."

"Do we have electricity here?"

"Yes. I checked that all out this morning."

Turning to David, Dan and Cindy, Carolyn said, "Let's get my tool box and some flashlights. I'll need those for crawling around under the floats."

It was cold in the old warehouse. Someone had clumsily tried to cover the hole in the roof with a tarpaulin. Beneath it stood what remained of Santa's sled and reindeers. Originally, the sled had been at the back of the float and four reindeer had been at the front in pairs, each carved out of plywood and painted.

Now there were deer heads and antlers strewn all over. The front of the sled had collapsed.

They all stood and watched as Carolyn walked around, inspecting the damage. Asking for a flashlight, Carolyn crawled under the back of the float to inspect its undercarriage.

Cindy shuddered at the idea of getting down on the cold floor and crawling around. David laughed. "That's my wife. Never happier than when she has a chance to crawl through cobwebs."

Dan gave him a nudge. "At least she's doing it on the floor. No ladders needed."

"Just give her a chance," David said glumly, "she'll no doubt have all of us up on them by the time she's finished. Every reindeer will have to be painted."

Cindy said, "What's this about ladders?"

"Ask David," Dan said with a grin.

But at that moment, Carolyn stood up, a smudge of dirt on her cheek and cobwebs caught on her bright red toque. Turning to Phil, she said, "I think we can save the undercarriage although I'd like Sam Forster to look at it just to make sure the axles and wheels are safe."

She walked around, testing the remains of reindeers and the sled. "Unfortunately, I think I'll have to re-build the sled and deer. Maybe we could have all eight and Rudolph this time. I wonder," she said, looking at David, "if there is some kind of motor or computer that could be used to make the deer go up and down."

David looked at Dan. "My darling wife doesn't exactly understand that I don't create computers. I'm just an idea man. However, I'll call on a few experts and find out what's on the market."

Dan nodded sympathetically. "It might be easier to use a simple little gas motor."

Ignoring the man-to-man sympathy, Carolyn said, "Dan, why don't you and Cindy go over to the other float and estimate the damage. I think I need to spend a little time explaining my idea to my darling husband."

Grinning, Dan and Cindy left David to deal with his wife's inspiration and headed over to the other float, flashlight in hand.

"You watch," Dan said. "She'll have David thinking up something."

Cindy laughed. He was right, of course. "What's this about ladders?" she asked. "Weren't you guys joking about them the other night, too?"

"You promise you'll never let on I told you?"

Really mystified now, Cindy said, "I promise."

"Well," Dan said as they reached the second float. "David is terrified of heights. Or at least he was. I think he's improved a little. He hates climbing ladders. Even worse, he can't stand seeing Carolyn up a ladder. I think he's had to come to terms with the fact that she's happiest when she's clambering up one but I don't think he finds it easy."

Cindy looked over at the pair just in time to see David attempting to help Carolyn as she scrambled up on the float to inspect the remains. "I see what you mean. I can see he isn't even comfortable with her climbing up on the float."

Looking at them, Dan could only agree. "I think David is to be admired. It must be difficult to give the one you love freedom to do what they want even when it scares you."

Moving away from him, she peered up over the edge of the float. "I haven't seen the parade for years. What exactly was on this one?"

"Well, the boards lying face down were the shape of a church. There was usually a Christmas tree at the other end and a small group of people standing around, usually in nineteenth-century costumes."

For a few minutes, they moved loose boards, examined the float base and Dan, with the help of a flashlight, the undercarriage. Crawling up and dusting himself off, Dan said, "I think the float is okay."

Just then, Carolyn came over and Dan reported their findings. Carolyn poked about a bit and said, "I think you're right. But I'll have to plan a new top for this float, too. Do you two think you could knock off all the pieces that are still standing? Anything you think we can use in the reconstruction, pile on the float. Phil's talked to Sam Forster. He's going to check the wheels and axles for safety. If they're okay, he's going to take the floats over to the lumber yard. They have an empty shed that's heated."

Carolyn looked at her watch. "It's almost eight right now. Do you think you could be finished by nine? Maybe we can go over to the coffee bar then."

Dan looked at Cindy and she nodded. "Okay, captain," he said to Carolyn. "We'll get to work."

Carolyn gave him an innocent smile, winked and then hurried off to deal with the other float. Hmm, he thought. Carolyn is trying to play Cupid. Turning to Cindy, he found her trying to hitch herself up on to the float. Before she could get her knee up on it, Dan was there. "Hey. There's an easier way. Turn around."

Cindy did, only to find herself staring at Dan's jacket. Before she quite figured out what was happening, he had her by the waist and lifted her up. "There you are, my lady." Then, he vaulted up on the float, held out his hand, and hoisted her to her feet.

Cindy quickly removed her hand and pretended to examine the wreck of what must have been the church. She was rattled. Touching him was like taking on a charge. When he'd lifted her up, all she was aware of was his nearness and his hands around her waist. With an effort she tried to concentrate on the float.

There had been a little path over a bridge between the spot where the Christmas trees had stood and the outline of the church. She was about to try and take the bridge apart when Dan said, "I think it would be easier if we worked together. Would you rather knock things with this mallet or hold them while I try to loosen them with it?"

"I'll hold, you hit."

They worked silently for a few minutes, slowly loosening the boards and placing them in a neat pile. "This reminds me of making the scenery for the play last summer," said Dan. "Only we were constructing rather than tearing things apart." Then he looked at her and smiled. "I remember the night I actually spoke to you for the first time. Carolyn, David and I had gone for coffee with the gang. You ended up sitting beside me."

Cindy was surprised. "You remember all that?"

Dan gave her an odd look. "Of course. Don't you?"

She was tempted to deny that she remembered the night. But there was something about the way he watched her that forced her tell the truth. "Yes, I remember. I thought you were Carolyn's boyfriend. I often saw you around town together. But that night, you didn't even seem to notice that she left with David."

With a funny look on his face, Dan attempted to sing, "But I only had eyes for you."

All Cindy's cynicism returned with a vengeance. She'd believed those words he sang until Gina had disillusioned her. She returned to her task, yanking at the boards, not waiting for Dan to loosen them. Suddenly, one came off, sending her back on her bottom. She automatically put down her hands to break her fall and felt a sharp pain.

"Ouch," she cried and sucked the pad of her hand below her thumb.

Dan was there in a second, taking her hand and staring at the wound. Glancing at his face, she saw that he'd gone pale. Looking down, she saw that whatever it was that she'd landed on had torn the pad of her hand. She grimaced and tried to free her hand.

Dan let go and grabbing both her arms, lifted her to her feet.

"Cindy, let me see that hand again."

By now, the blood was welling out of a rather nasty wound. He reached in his pocket and pulled out some clean tissues. Folding them in a pad, and holding her hand still, he pressed the tissues on the wound. Then he looked around. To his dismay, he realized she must have fallen against the point of a rusty nail protruding out of the base of the bridge.

"When did you last have a tetanus shot?" he asked.

Cindy was feeling a little queasy now and her hand was starting to really hurt. "I don't know. Can't remember. Maybe years ago when I cut myself on some glass when playing baseball."

"Here," Dan said, "sit on the side of the float. I'll jump down and lift you to the floor."

Cindy couldn't believe her own reaction to the wound. She let Dan ease her down so her feet hung over the float and then was only too glad when he lifted her to the floor. "Come on," he said. "We're going to the clinic. I think you need stitches. You definitely need a tetanus shot."

Cindy hated needles and the thought of stitches was

enough to have her tossing her supper up. "Can't we go back to your clinic? Can't you do it?"

Now why had she said that? But before she could answer her own question, Dan had his arm around her shoulders and was hurrying her over to Carolyn and David.

"We're going over to the clinic. It's open until nine. Cindy has torn her hand on a nail."

And then before they could do or say a thing, Dan picked Cindy up in his arms and said, "Open the door for us. David, my keys are in my pocket. See if you can get them out and unlock the four by four. Do you have your phone with you?"

David pulled the keys from his pocket. Carolyn called, "I do. I'll phone the clinic and tell them you're coming."

When they got in the vehicle, Dan rooted around in his case and found a pad and bandage. Quickly he applied the pad and taped it onto her hand. "Hold that tight, Cindy," he instructed and headed off to the clinic.

There were two people waiting to see the doctor when Dan strode in. The nurse Helen Baines led them into an examining room.

Dan eased Cindy to her feet and said, "Here, let me take your coat and hat off." Then, he lifted her up to sit on the examining table.

By now, Cindy realized that Dan was quite upset. He looked grey. She was just about to ask him if he was alright when the doctor, Jim Anderson, walked in.

"What's this I hear about an accident?" he asked.

Before Cindy could speak, Dan said, "Cindy fell and her hand landed on a rusty nail. It tore her palm. And she can't remember when she last had a tetanus shot."

The doctor took her hand and carefully removed the bandage. He squeezed the pad of her hand gently and she could see that the injury was rather deep. She looked away from it.

"Are you okay?" the doctor asked. "You're not feeling faint, are you?"

Cindy shook her head. "No, I just feel a little nauseous."

"I'm going to have to clean this wound and put in a stitch or so. Then I'll give you a tetanus shot and something for the pain. If you give your hand a rest for a few days, it will be as good as new."

The doctor had Cindy move to a chair and put her hand on his desk. After he had cleaned it, he got up and prepared a needle to freeze the area. I hate this, Cindy thought with a shudder. When the doctor sat down and checked the needle, she turned her head away just in time to see Dan's eyes roll up in his head as he slumped to the floor.

The doctor held her wrist still and barked, "Helen. I need you in here right now."

Cindy frantically tried to wiggle loose and get to Dan. "What's happened to him?"

At this point, the nurse hurried in. Without waiting for instructions, she checked his pulse, then grinned. "He's fine. Who'd have believed Dr. Dan would faint at the sight of a needle."

As the doctor slickly eased the needle into Cindy's hand, he said, "I've seen Dan get a needle with the best of them and he's never fainted." Looking right at Cindy and winking, he said, "I think the circumstances might just have something to do with it. While we're waiting for the freezing to take I'll see to Dan."

* * *

Helen was just returning to her desk when Carolyn and David hurried into the office. "We've come to see how your patient is."

"Patients," Helen said.

"Patients?" David asked.

Helen ginned. "Doc said you were to go in. He thought he might need a hand."

Mystified, the two of them knocked and then entered the examining room. The doctor was placing a bandage on Cindy's hand. Dan was on the floor, a blanket over him and a pillow under his head.

"Heavens," Carolyn said. "What's wrong with Dan?"

"Don't worry," the doctor said. "He just passed out at the sight of the needle. We've checked him. He's alright." Nodding at Cindy, he said, "We both thought it might be a good idea if I finished working on her hand and gave her the tetanus shot before urging him back to the present."

"But Jim," Carolyn said, "I've seen Dan get a shot without flinching. And he certainly gives enough of them."

Glancing over at Cindy, he said, "I think the situation is just a little different this time."

"What do you mean?" asked Cindy.

"You'll figure it out, in time."

Cindy was still frowning when he gave her the tetanus shot. The minute he was finished, Cindy was on her knees beside Dan.

Placing her hand on his forehead, she looked accusingly at the doctor and said, "His head is cold."

"Means he's got no fever," the doctor replied.

But she wasn't listening to him. She took one of Dan's hands with her good one. "Dan. Dan. Wake up."

At that, Dan's lashes fluttered and finally, his eyes

opened. Looking around, he saw Cindy beside him and Carolyn and David peering down.

"What happened?"

The doctor said, "You fainted." Leaning over, he took his arm. "Come on, Dan. Sit up slowly."

As Dan struggled to sit up, he said indignantly, "I've never fainted in my life." He shook his head in disbelief and then he noticed Cindy's hand. "Oh," he said.

"*Oh* is right. It was a classic faint," the doctor said with relish. "Your eyes rolled up in your head and you slumped down as gracefully as a ballet dancer doing the dying swan. Didn't even make a thump. Isn't that right, Cindy?"

Cindy was still mystified. Why was everyone including the doctor making a big joke about this? Before she could start to complain, the doctor said, "Carolyn. Could you help Cindy on with her jacket and then I'll put on a sling just to keep her hand up until it stops hurting."

Going over to a cupboard, he got a small container of pills. "Take two of these before you go to bed so you can get a good night's sleep. Your hand should be fine in the morning. Now, scram, the bunch of you. There are still two patients waiting to see me."

As they headed for their respective vehicles, David said, "Why don't you all come back to the house and we'll have some hot chocolate or tea or whatever is good for shock. I think it might be a good idea if Cindy stayed with us again. I'll drive the SUV over for you. Carolyn can take Cindy in the truck."

For once, neither Dan nor Cindy felt like arguing.

When they reached the Reids', Carolyn and David settled Dan and Cindy before the fireplace, made tea and put out goodies left over from the house-warming. Valiantly, the two of them tried to get a conversation going but it soon became apparent that Dan's mind was off somewhere else. He sat there with a slight frown on his face most of the time and only seemed to hear half of what they were saying. Cindy was just as bad. She sipped her tea and watched the rest of them but didn't seem inclined to talk. It wasn't until the color came back to Cindy's cheeks that her interest picked up. She asked, "Carolyn, have you any ideas for the floats now?"

"Sure do," Carolyn replied. "Just a moment until I get my sketch pad."

David teased, "She thought you'd never ask."

Carolyn returned and began to sketch. "I think we should have all nine reindeer and that they should look like they're just arriving. Santa's sled has to be the highest part and will hang out over the back of the float base. Somehow, we have to get the effect of the reindeer flying in to land without them really moving very much."

She held up her sketch for them all to see. Rudolph had just landed while the other pairs of deer were angled up in the air behind him. Santa's sled was at the highest point on the float.

There was silence while they examined her drawing. Finally, David held up his hands so his wrists touched and then moved his hands up and down so that when one was down the other was up and vice versa. "I'm not the mechanical one here, however, I have an idea. If you have the deer in pairs and could somehow move first the left-hand deer and then the right-hand deer up and down, it might give the illusion of flight."

Carolyn threw her hands around his neck and rewarded him with a kiss. "Darling, you're a genius."

Dan caught on immediately. "All you'd need would be two small gas engines with pulleys. Each engine would drive one line of deer. You'd have to set the timing so that one line of deer went up while the other was coming down."

Carolyn clapped her hands with delight. "Brilliant."

Dan looked hopeful. "Do I get a kiss, too?"

Carolyn looked as if she was about to leap across the coffee table separating them when David put an arm around her shoulder. "Hold it right there. Let him get his own wife to reward him."

Dan grinned. "It was worth a try."

At this point, Cindy was unable to hide a yawn. Immediately, Carolyn felt guilty. "Cindy, I'm sorry. You must be bushed and your hand is probably hurting. Take your pills and I'll go up with you to make sure the room is fine. I still haven't changed the bed. I must have known you'd need it again."

Cindy took her pills and then turned to Dan. "Thanks for looking after me, Dan. I'm really sorry you fainted. I hope you're feeling alright." Getting up, she followed Carolyn out of the room.

The minute Cindy left, Charlie the cat jumped up on the sofa and settled himself on Dan's lap. Amused, Dan said, "It looks like he's forgiven me."

He stroked the cat for a few moments and looked moodily into the fire. Finally, he looked at David. "I've got to apologize for teasing you about your reaction every time Carolyn goes up ladders. Suddenly it's no longer a joke. I know exactly how you feel. When I saw that gash on Cindy's hand, I thought I was going to throw up. And when Jim aimed that needle at her hand, I was lost."

David smiled. "Apology accepted. It's funny, Carolyn's dad told me when he'd heard about my little problem that he'd known immediately that I was in love with her long before I knew it myself."

Dan rubbed Charlie's ear, a frown still on his face. "But what if Cindy's life had depended on me doing something about her wound? I'm afraid I'd repeat tonight's performance."

David shook his head. "I'm sure you wouldn't. After all, you put a pad on her hand immediately, even before you got to your case in the car. And you were very quick in getting her to a doctor."

"I hope you're right." Stifling a yawn, Dan said, "I think I'd better get back to the clinic. I have a surgery at eight tomorrow."

As they both stood, David asked, "How are things going between you and Cindy?"

Dan frowned. "I have no idea." Then straightening, he asserted, "However, I intend to discover why she disappeared so suddenly out of my life last summer. I think the least she owes me is an explanation."

David slapped him on the back. "That's the spirit."

As they headed to the SUV, he said, "Oh, I just remembered. I wanted to ask you if you would consider taking the puppy that Cindy hit. He seems intelligent and sweet-natured. He's still very young so you'd be able to train him easily."

"I'd like to see him first before I decide," David said.

"Of course. Come in any time."

"Have you given him a name yet?"

"Cindy did. She called him Crash."

David laughed. "Great name. There is just one problem. I'd like the puppy to be a surprise on Christmas morning."

"Quite frankly, I don't think he'll be ready to go to a home before that. The injury to his lung and ribs was fairly serious. However, he's making excellent progress. I'm sure he'll be none the worse for the accident. I'll gladly keep him for you. I'd enjoy the company."

David thought for a moment. "I'd really like to take him. I think Carolyn would want the puppy to have a home. I'll come in some time this week and meet him."

Dan opened the door and swung up into the Pathfinder. "Thank Carolyn for suggesting that Cindy stay overnight."

David shrugged. "We're happy to have her. Oh, by the way. How about the dog's expenses? It must be costing a bundle to treat and keep him."

Dan said, "It's all taken care of. Cindy wanted to pay for the puppy's care. We worked out a deal. She can cater for my open house and we'll call it even. And don't worry, I intend to see that she isn't bankrupted buying supplies."

David grinned. "That was a clever move."

Carolyn watched Cindy as she ate her breakfast. There were dark circles beneath her eyes. "Did your hand keep you awake last night?"

"Not at first. I slept until about four o'clock. Then I must have moved. Maybe I hit it or put my weight on it because the pain woke me up. I got up and took another pill in that very glamorous ensuite bathroom. Carolyn, you treat your guests like royalty."

"I'm glad you like it. Now, tell me, is that hand going to interfere with your test cooking?"

Cindy held up her hand and looked at the bandage. Her fingers were free but not her thumb. "Doc Anderson said I should keep the bandage around my thumb until tomorrow. By then, he thinks the healing will be established and using it won't weaken the stitches. Anyway, my project isn't working out. It is far too complicated to be properly done by the time school begins. I'll have to think of something else."

Cindy took a sip of her coffee and then asked, "Why do you think Dan fainted last night? I saw him deal with someone's cut hand last summer without turning a hair."

Carolyn said gently, "He didn't care for the person last summer."

Cindy pulled a face. "Why would you think he cares for me? I told you all about Gina."

Carolyn looked smug. "Dan acted just like David does when I head up a ladder. David says it makes his head swim and his heart rate increase."

Cindy shoved her coffee mug about. "Then why did he take up with Gina? She insinuated they had a some kind of relationship. She went on a weekend to Ottawa with him."

"Maybe you should ask him why he did. Or maybe he didn't realize he was in love with you then."

Cindy rolled her eyes. It was easier to do this than speak. Tears were just too near the surface. Finishing her coffee, she stood up.

"Dan phoned before you were awake. He said he had a call to make at a farm about a mile down the road. He thought he'd be finished by ten-thirty and offered to pick you up and take you in to see the puppy. Hope you don't mind. It would save me a trip to town. I'm in the middle of drawing a template for the deer and I'd really like to finish it. David's gone to Smithboro to get some special supplies for the floats."

Looking at her watch, Cindy saw that it was after ten. "I'd better get hopping. Thanks again for putting me up." Then she had a thought. "Do you think you and David will still be able to manage to come for supper on Tuesday?"

Carolyn looked at the calendar hanging in the kitchen. "I have it marked in. I hope to have things ready so that the gang can start painting on Wednesday. I'm sure that all the construction will be finished by Tuesday afternoon. I'll be glad of a break."

Just then, a vehicle came up the lane. Glancing out the window, Cindy saw Dan getting out of his vehicle. "I'll just get my coat," said Cindy.

Going toward the door, Carolyn said, "Let's see if Dan can stop for a moment." She opened the door and waited while Dan stamped the slush off his boots and entered the mud room. "Do you have time for some coffee?" she asked.

Loosening his jacket, Dan said, "I'd love a quick one." Then moving into the dining area, he saw Cindy. "How's the hand today?"

She still had it in her sling. "It's fine as long as I keep it up in the sling. I think by tomorrow, I'll be back to normal."

All three of them sat down while Dan sipped his coffee and attacked a dish of cookies. "Boy, that's just what I needed. I had a surgery at eight and then a farm call at nine so it's been a rush. However, that's soon to end. I had a message on my phone last night to call Merry."

When Carolyn looked puzzled, Dan explained. "Dr. Meredith Harper, my new associate. Cindy met her the other morning. Anyway, Merry phoned to say that she could begin on Monday."

"What is she going to do with her little boy?" Cindy asked.

"Merry's parents are coming to stay at her house

and look after the little guy for the next few weeks. Merry will go home on the weekends or arrange for her son and parents to come up here."

"How old is the little boy?" asked Carolyn.

"He's four, and in case you're wondering, Merry is a widow. Her husband was killed several years ago. She's anxious to live in a small village like Stewart's Falls. Thinks it will be a good place to bring up a youngster."

"Where's she going to stay?" Cindy asked.

"She said she looked up bed and breakfasts on the Internet and read about Cliffside B&B. They had a suite she could use. They also have more accommodation if her parents want to come up with her son. They may do that for the Santa Claus parade."

Dan took the last cookie from the plate and polished it off with his coffee. "By the way, Carolyn, Merry wondered if there was a house to rent in the village. I figured you'd know."

Carolyn thought for a moment. "Not that I'm aware of."

Dan frowned at that. "That's too bad. I'm anxious Merry should get settled somewhere as soon as possible. I want her to feel that this is just the place for her to begin her new life."

"I have an idea," said Cindy, "but I'll have to check it out."

Both Carolyn and Dan looked at her in surprise.

She explained. "My parents plan to stay in Florida until the end of April. They really prefer someone to stay in their house. It's got lots of space. She could even have a housekeeper live in if she wanted."

Dan asked, "Would you phone them when you get home and ask? That would be the perfect solution."

*   *   *

Dan watched Cindy as she approached the puppy's cage. She called softly, "Hi there, Crash. How's the leg today?"

The puppy struggled to sit up. He wiggled forward so that he could put his nose against the wire.

"You can open the cage," Dan said.

Cindy carefully opened the door and the puppy licked her fingers. "He's a lovely puppy. I do so hope he gets a good home."

"I think I may have found one already."

Cindy gave him a radiant smile that he felt all the way to his toes. "You have?"

"David was looking for a puppy for a Christmas present for Carolyn. He said he'd come and check out Crash. I'm pretty sure he'll like him. Don't say anything to anyone about it. I'd like David to be sure he wants him."

Carolyn ruffled the puppy's coat. "But what will you do with Crash until then?"

"I'll keep him here with me. When that rib injury is really healed, he can stay with me in the apartment when I'm in. He's used to a cage now so he'll be alright when I'm working."

Cindy turned to him and for a moment, he thought she was going to throw her arms around him. But she paused mid-motion and said huskily, "You're a good person, Dan. I'll never be able to thank you enough."

Crossing an invisible line that had kept them apart since she'd returned, he reached out and touched her cheek. "I didn't do it for thanks, Cindy. I did it because I wanted you to be happy."

She caught his hand and held it. For a moment, they both forgot the puppy, then Gina walked in and stepped briskly over to Dan. Standing far too close, as far as Cindy was concerned. Gina said, "The druggist just called. He said he saw a very young puppy the same age and color as Crash digging around in the garbage behind the neighboring restaurant. It was very wary. He couldn't get it to come to him."

Cindy said, "I can't understand how someone could raise those puppies and then just dump them."

Dan went over and shut the cage. "Come on. I'll drive you out to your house. It's started to thaw outside. I'd like to be sure your lane is safe and that the deck is clean. You don't want to be pushing or shoveling snow until that hand heals. Then I'll take a look around town for the puppy."

Cindy was about to object. Then she noticed the sour look on Gina's face and changed her mind. "Thanks, I'd appreciate the ride."

Pleased that he'd won that round, Dan added, "Maybe you could phone your parents while I'm doing that and ask them about renting the house to Merry after you go back to town."

"That's a good idea."

When they went out to the car, they couldn't help but notice the effect of the thaw. Water was pooling where the sidewalk was shoveled and as they walked along the lane to the car, their footsteps filled with moisture.

Dan helped Cindy up into the SUV and then slipped behind the steering wheel. "It's going to be messy driving," observed Cindy. "I hope my back road is okay."

Dan bowed his head toward her. "I promise, Miss Worrywart, to drive sedately."

Cindy was about to poke him and then remembered her hand. Instead she folded her hands and looked prim. Dan laughed and she felt good.

* * *

Cindy placed the telephone back on the receiver and went to the door. As she'd been talking to her parents, she watched Dan out the window clearing off the heavy snow she'd left on the deck and making a place for the water to run away so it didn't pool on the path from the garage to the house. Now, he was squinting at the roof.

When she opened the door, Dan called, "I should have come out here and shoveled off your roof. For early December, we've had an unusual amount of snow and it's all piled up on this side. The wind must blow it around the house so it drifts up there."

Cindy rolled her eyes. "Dan Hamilton. Don't ever let me catch you up on that roof during the winter. If you slipped, you'd fall two stories."

Dan placed his hand over his heart and said, "Beautiful maiden, you'd care?"

Ignoring the 'beautiful', Cindy said, "Of course I'd care."

Dan mumbled something like, "Then I'd better get climbing."

Questioning her hearing, Cindy demanded, "What did you say?"

"I said I'd better get going."

"Oh."

Dan took the shovel over to the garage and was about to start for the SUV when Cindy remembered her telephone call. "I talked to my parents."

Dan hurried back. "What did they say?"

"They said they'd be glad to rent the house if Merry and they can agree on a suitable rent. They suggested that she come and see the house and then, if she's interested, she can telephone them and work out the details."

Dan grabbed her by the arms and swung her around.

"Cindy, you're an angel." Then for good measure, he kissed her lightly on the lips and put her down. Before she could quite recover from the spin and the kiss, he said, "Look. Let's celebrate by going for dinner. I have to see a patient out near The Pines. It has an excellent dining room in the main lodge. I could pick you up and take you with me when I see the patient, then we could go out for dinner."

When she looked doubtful, he said, "Come on, Cindy. You can't use that hand today. And," he added, "they're known for the food. It'll give you a chance to check out the local talent."

Cindy wanted to ask why he wanted to spend so much time with her. She wanted to ask him if he was going to treat her as he had last summer, taking up with someone else the moment she was off the scene. She was about to refuse but something in Dan's eyes, some sense that this was very important to him, made her agree.

For a moment he looked as if he was going to spin her around again but instead, he hurried to the SUV. "I'll pick you up about four. That will give me time to see my patient on the way and then drive up to the lodge."

As Cindy walked back into the house, dodging the dripping of icicles as she went in the door, she realized that she wasn't sure just how casual or dressy the dining room was. Going to the telephone, she dialed Carolyn.

The phone rang four times before Carolyn answered. Unbeknownst to Cindy, Carolyn nearly levitated when she heard that Dan was taking her to The Pines. Instead, she said, "Cindy, you'll love The Pines. David and I have had some very special meals there. Dress is dressy casual."

When Cindy hung up, Carolyn couldn't resist running up the stairs from her basement workshop where she kept her large electric tools and hurrying into David's study. He was standing at a window looking out over the frozen lake when he heard her coming. He turned in time to catch her flying into his arms. "Just guess," she bubbled. "Dan's taking Cindy to The Pines tonight."

He hugged her for a moment, then put her down and said, "Turn around."

"Whatever for?" she asked.

He took her shoulders and steered her around. Then he fingered her shoulder blades.

Squinting her eyes and turning her head to try to see, she said, "What on earth are you doing?"

Laughing, he said, "Just wondering if you'd grown wings."

Carolyn pulled a face. "Come on, admit it. You're just as pleased as I am."

David put his arm over her shoulder and steered her toward the kitchen. "I feel like a cup of tea." And then he added, "You've got to admire Dan. He certainly knows the moves. Taking Cindy to The Pines and finding a way to save her from an expensive veterinary bill. Not bad."

As they had tea, he explained how Dan had bargained with Cindy.

The road into The Pines followed the edge of the lake on which the building was situated. The last of the sunset touched the mist that hovered over the melted surface of the lake, creating a luminous lilac haze between the dark frame of the tall pines and the silhouette of the leafless birches and maples.

When they rounded the last curve of the road they

came upon the lodge. Its windows cast light onto the shadows of the great pines that framed it. Behind the lodge a high wall of granite loomed, its peak catching the last rays of the sun.

"What a beautiful setting," said Cindy.

Dan nodded. "Let's sit here and watch until the sun has completely set."

As he watched her enjoy the scene he worried. To-night had been an impulse. Would he regret it? Could he get any closer to the truth of what had separated them? So much depended upon the right words. What if they ended up farther apart?

Finally, it was dark and they left the car to follow the path to the entrance. It opened into the lodge's reception area. Dan helped Cindy out of a short camel coat he'd never seen on her before, tucked her blue silk scarf in the sleeve and hung it up for her.

"You aren't wearing the sling tonight. Your hand must be feeling better."

Cindy held up the hand for his perusal. "I've freed my thumb and if I'm careful, I don't feel the stitches pull."

He held the arm of her injured hand while she balanced herself and pulled off her snow boots. He was enchanted when she slipped her feet into a pair of delicate tan pumps. He thought she was lovely. Her riot of curls were held back somehow behind her ears. She wore a creamy silk shirt with camel-colored slacks. Gold earrings and a gold chain completed the outfit.

At his inspection, she said nervously, "I hope I'm dressed appropriately."

"You look perfect," Dan said as he shrugged off his coat and hung it. He wore a tweed jacket with soft touches of blue in the weave. His grey trousers and blue silk tie picked up the greys and blues of his jacket. Holding out his arm, he said, "Let's go and see what the chef has for us tonight."

A large stone fireplace extended across one end of the dining room. The flames of the fire illuminated the huge squared logs that made the walls. Over the mantle an autumn scene painted in oils flamed out at them. Heavy wrought-iron lamps hung on circular frames high up in the room while on each table, iron holders held candles.

The owner led them to a table by a window where they could appreciate the fire but still be private. He presented them with parchment paper menus and left them to make their choices.

Cindy was intrigued with the idea of parchment paper for a menu. She looked at the front and back and admired the calligraphy. Dan was amused. "I thought you'd be more interested in the contents than the design."

She smoothed her finger across the paper surface, trying to decide if the words were handwritten or done on a computer. "I'm always interested in the way restaurants present their menus," she explained. Looking around, she examined the dining room. The decorator had chosen plain pine tables and chairs. Covering the tables were crisp white tablecloths on which sat handwoven placemats picking up the colors of the oil painting. Touching one, she said, "These were made in New Brunswick by a well-known weaver." Picking up a sturdy pressed glass goblet, she commented, "They've been very clever. Instead of using crystal, they've got either replicas of early pressed glass goblets or the actual thing."

Giving him one of those smiles that melted his insides, she said, "Thank you for bringing me here. It is a perfectly lovely room."

At last she looked at the menu. There were only three entrees offered. Similarly, the choice of soup and appetizer was limited. "I think the food is going to be just as good as I've heard it is. The chef's been smart enough to offer only a few things so he can concentrate on quality. I bet they handwrite a new menu every day."

They each had the same soup; a wonderful concoction of leeks and carrots. Cindy selected poached salmon while Dan chose a rack of lamb. As they waited for their soup, Cindy cupped her hands to the window and looked out. "It's going to be beautiful, Dan. I can already see the evening star and the sliver of a new moon. By Christmas time, it should be a full moon. Let's hope it snows again. Snow always looks so beautiful in the moonlight."

The food was everything Dan could have wished. To his delight, Cindy was completely entranced with each offering. As they ate, they talked in generalities; the puppy, the floats Carolyn was repairing, the fun they would have when they met with the rest of their friends to paint the floats.

Over coffee, Dan asked, "Cindy, tell me about this term at school. Has it been everything you hoped?"

She was surprised at this question. "Are you sure you really want to know?"

"I'd like to understand what your career means to you."

For a few moments, Cindy thought about his request. Finally, she said, "I don't think describing the course will answer your question. But I could tell you why I like working with food."

"I'd like that very much."

"I feel like an artist when I work with food. As I've gained experience, I've found that I can create beautiful things. The beauty isn't just the appearance. It's in the taste and the texture of the food, too. And it's so much fun to try to be original."

Cindy's eyes sparkled with enthusiasm in the soft candlelight. How could he compete with such dedication? he wondered. Maybe she left Stewart's Falls so suddenly last summer because she wanted to travel and study cooking all over the world? Funny, he hadn't thought of that before. He should have. It was a natural explanation. But surely she would have talked to him about such a decision. To just leave seemed more and more out of character.

Picking up something in Dan's expression, she faltered. "I'm sorry. I must be boring you."

"You're not boring me. I asked how you felt. I wanted to hear about your plans."

"Why?" she asked.

"Because I'm interested."

At that, Cindy looked down and played with the cutlery left on the table. Taking courage in his hand, Dan asked the question he most wanted answered. "Cindy, where do you see yourself giving vent to all this creativity when you're through school?"

Cindy turned her water goblet and watched the candlelight reflected in the glass's design. Last summer, she'd thought of settling in Stewart's Falls, maybe opening a tearoom. Suddenly, that dream seemed important again. Then she smiled at him and said, "I think I would really love to open a tearoom serving lunch and afternoon tea."

Now came the second most difficult question for Dan to ask. "Where would you want to have your tearoom? Toronto?"

Cindy shook her head, her curls golden in the candlelight. "No. I think I would like to have a tearoom in a small town or village. Possibly one that has a good tourist trade in the summer but also enough local people who would enjoy it in the winter."

Dan gave a silent cheer. "Just for fun, let's pretend you were looking for such a place in Stewart's Falls. What kind of location would you be looking for?"

Cindy was enjoying herself now. Just talking about her plans made them seem clearer. "I'd like to find an older house, either just off the main street or maybe on the edge of town. It would be nice if patrons could walk to it. Of course, other people might come from the countryside for lunch on the days when they come to shop."

Slowly, Dan was getting the picture. "How big a dining room would you need?"

"Well, I think I'd only want to sit about twenty-four people. It's better not to have too large an area or one would have to have more staff."

"I'm trying to imagine such an older house," said Dan.

Cindy shut her eyes and tried to clarify her vision. "Maybe one with a glassed-in sun porch. In the summer, you could open the windows and serve some of the patrons there. In the winter, the room could still be used but it would have to have double-glazed windows. I'd use the living room and maybe the dining room as the eating areas, too. I'd also want one of the rooms to have a fireplace. There would have to be room for a working kitchen, washrooms and maybe even a room for selling local crafts."

"Stewart's Falls could use such a place, Cindy."

Cindy sat back and studied Dan. Was he suggesting

she stick around after dismissing her so easily before? She wished she could read his mind.

Just then, the owner came over with the bill. Dan gave him his credit card and then looked at his watch. "Cindy. It's almost ten o'clock. I didn't mean to keep you up so late. I'm sure your hand must be hurting."

Cindy looked at her hand. Now that he mentioned it, it was. But she hadn't noticed the discomfort until he drew her attention to it. "My hand really hasn't bothered me. Surely you could tell. I ate every bit of that wonderful supper."

As they walked out of the dining room, Dan couldn't resist steering her through the tables, his hand lightly on her waist. He missed the closeness he'd felt with her in the summer.

Outside, the air was balmy and a long sliver of grey mist remained over the lake. But above it the sky was clear, the stars diamond sharp, the tiny moon a fragile crescent. As they reached the SUV, a star plummeted across the sky.

"Make a wish," they both cried at the same time and then laughed.

Cindy said, "I hope mine comes true."

Taking her hand, Dan said, "I hope mine does, too."

As they returned to the SUV, Dan realized that time was running out. He had to ask his question now. Holding the door open for Cindy, he said, "Why did you disappear last summer?"

Cindy couldn't believe he'd asked the question. *He* expected *her* to tell him what he already knew? She slipped up on to the seat and snapped her seatbelt shut angrily. When Dan got in the vehicle, he found her sitting with her back straight, staring out the window.

Starting the SUV, he asked again, "Why, Cindy?"

She turned to him and he could see that she was furious. "You need to ask?"

Now what in the earth did that mean? How could he figure out what had gone wrong if she wouldn't even talk about it?

Aware that the interior of the SUV was pulsing with unspoken, incomprehensible feelings all generating from Cindy, Dan decided to wait until they got to her place. The minute the SUV came to a stop, Cindy unhooked her seat belt, opened the door and hopped out. In a very cool, polite voice, she said, "Thanks for the lovely supper, Dan. In response to your question, consider this question. Did you have a nice time with Gina in Ottawa?"

Then she slammed the door and headed toward the house.

Dan was out of the SUV and up on the deck in a flash. "What are you talking about?"

Turning to him, she said, "Well, didn't you go to Ottawa with Gina?"

"Of course, I went to Ottawa with Gina. So what?"

Fumbling with her key, Cindy said, "Just forget it."

Suddenly, Dan began to see the light. She was jealous. She thought Gina and he had taken a holiday together. Now he was really annoyed. After all they had shared last summer, she thought he would take up with someone else?

Pulling her around to face him, he said, "Look at me."

Furious, Cindy tried to pull away but Dan caught her chin and made her look at him.

"This is about trust, Cindy. You didn't trust me last summer, not even enough to ask." Releasing her and striding angrily back to the SUV, he called over his shoulder, "Forget I asked the question. I thought what we had last summer was special but it obviously wasn't."

Getting in the SUV, he slammed the door, started the vehicle and roared down the road.

Shaken beyond belief, Cindy leaned her forehead against the door and wept. What Dan said was true. She hadn't trusted him. Instead, she'd let Gina make her jealous. She'd swallowed every story Gina had trotted out.

Struggling to see through her tears, she finally got the key in the lock and the door opened. Like a zombie, she rebuilt the fire, turned off the lights and headed for bed, sure she had destroyed the one true love she would ever have.

Chapter Four

Cindy woke in the middle of the night only to remember the terrible argument she'd had with Dan. Groaning, she sat up and turned on the light. Only then did she realize she still had her clothes on. She'd thrown herself on her bed when she'd come in and cried herself to sleep. Now, everything was wrinkled. Her eyes were gritty from weeping.

She was exhausted, too tired to shower. Fumbling with her clothes, she managed to get out of them, pull on a long T-shirt and stumble back to bed. Turning off the light, she turned on her side and tried to sleep but memories haunted her. She and Dan had paired off from the moment they'd met in the coffee shop but at first, it had been just a friendship. Slowly, as they flirted, played tennis and met after play rehearsals, her feelings for Dan had grown more serious. Many an evening they'd talked as they'd walked across the park and along the river, sharing their interests and telling stories about their families, their childhoods and finally their dreams. But at no time was love mentioned. No kisses, no caresses. It was as if neither of them wanted to spoil what they had by taking the risk of declaring their feelings and being rejected.

Cindy had had the lead in a farce that summer. Almost everyone was taking part in it; either acting or working on the scenery and props. About two weeks before the performance, Cindy was still trying to learn her lines. Meeting Dan after a very frustrating rehearsal, Cindy told him about her problem. Without blinking an eye, Dan said, "Can you get tomorrow off?"

"Sure, why do you ask?"

"It's my day off. I'll help you learn the lines. We could take a picnic and go out to Crescent Lake. I know where there is a small beach. It's a weekday and still June so it will likely be deserted." With a grin, Dan added, "I'll feed you the lines. You can feed me lunch."

They arrived at the long thin lake the next morning at ten-thirty. Dan brought two director's chairs, a blanket and a small cooler of fruit juice. Cindy brought a basket of food; nothing fancy since she'd had no time to cook.

They set up the stage on the tiny beach and attempted to work through the scenes she was having difficulty with. Much of the farce was sheer nonsense with characters coming in and out of doors and hiding in closets. Of course there was a villain who wanted the heroine Rosette. He tried every trick in the book to remove the hero Roger from circulation.

They were exhausted from laughing by the time they came to the last scene when Roger finally gets the girl. When the scene opens, Rosette thinks Roger has been killed by the villain.

They set up the scene. A huge boulder served as a chair for Rosette. The surrounding scene was a garden. Humming to himself, Dan picked up buttercups and small white daisies and stuck them into the sand. Then, they began.

Cindy settled herself on the rock. She spread out an imaginary skirt and then with the play in one hand, she began.

ROSETTE: (*Rocking back and forth and crying dramatically*) **Boo hoo. He's gone. I'm sure he's dead. Whatever will I do?**
Getting right into the spirit of the scene, Dan overemphasizes every gesture Roger makes.

ROGER: (*picking up a bouquet of daisies and buttercups from the sand creeps up behind Rosette and listens*)

ROSETTE: (*moans*) **I didn't tell him I love him.** (*She sniffs and blows her nose loudly into a large handkerchief*) You can hear Cindy right across the lake.

ROGER: (*Tickles her cheek with the flowers*) **Tell who, my love?**

ROSETTE: (*She jumps up, her mouth a round O the audience can see and turns around*)
Roger, oh Roger. You're alive. (*She throws herself into his arms*) Cindy leaps off the rock.

ROGER: (*He staggers but manfully manages to catch Rosette*) **Who do you love, my dearest?**
Dan sputters under the force of Cindy's impact.

ROSETTE: **You, Roger.** (*They kiss a long, dramatic stage kiss*) What begins as a stage kiss deepens rapidly to the real thing.

Suddenly the farce is over and reality takes hold. They both step back from the kiss, clearly shaken.

Dan whispered, "I've been wanting to do that for days," and cupping her head, proceeded to kiss her again; her forehead, her cheeks, the tip of her nose and finally, her lips. If the last kiss lit a fire, this one ignited an explosion. When it ended, Cindy murmured, "You're making up the lines" and pulled his head back down. This time, the kiss was everything a kiss should be; passionate yet tender, demanding yet giving.

Finally, they came up for air and stood facing each other. Nervously, Cindy shoved a curl behind her ear. She didn't know what to say. That kiss had definitely taken them into new territory.

Seeing her confusion and knowing she needed time, Dan reached out and took her hand. "Come on," he said gently. "Let's eat."

They spread the food out on the blanket under a pine tree. As they ate, they talked but the conversation was full of pauses, of unasked questions until Dan finally reached over and took the cookie she was anxiously crumbling and said, "I'm in love with you, Cindy. I have been since the first time I saw you. I realize that it is probably the last thing you want to happen this summer."

Cindy brushed the cookie crumbs from her shorts, then, still looking down, she said softly, "It is the last thing I thought would ever happen, you in love with me. It's too much like a fairy tale come true. I feel just the same way. . . ."

Cindy rolled over in her bed and clutched a pillow to her. She'd had her heart's desire and now she'd ruined everything.

Still holding the pillow, she finally fell asleep.

*   *   *

Cindy stretched and turned over in bed, not asleep yet not quite awake. She was dreaming that she was busy fixing up an old-fashioned Victorian sun porch. She'd furnished it with white rattan chairs and tables with circular glass tops. In her dreamlike state, she tried to choose fabric to cover the chair seats in her sunroom which was also a decorator's store. The fabric bolts were tremendously high, and as she tried to pick one she liked, they all began to topple off the display rack; plop, plop, plop.

Frantic to pick them up before Dan, the store manager, found the display in shambles, Cindy began hoisting them back on the rack. As she placed one at one end of the rack, another would fall; plop.

Agitated in her semi-conscious state, she turned over again when a plop brought her suddenly awake. Water. On her face! In a state of confusion, she sat up and shook her head. Water splashed on the tip of her nose.

Wide awake now, she jumped out of bed and looked up. There, to her horror, was a wet patch on the ceiling and in the center of the spot a large drip of water was forming, ready to plop.

Cindy yanked the bed away from the path of the drop and rushed to the washroom. Grabbing towels and the waste paper basket, she placed the towels down to try to soak up the moisture and then put the basket right under the drip. She could see that it was going to fill quickly.

Pulling back the curtains, she looked out the window. The sun sparkled off large icicles that were hanging from the eaves and dripping to the ground a floor below. The snow that had come so early in the season was melting. Obviously, the snow on the roof was also melting and pooling up under the shingles from the layer of ice that fed the icicles.

For a few moments, all thought of her argument with Dan was forgotten. Grabbing her clothing, she hurried into the bathroom, quickly washed and dressed, and headed down the stairs. She found a large plastic garbage container to replace the small bathroom one and then considered how to get help.

Her first instinct was to phone Dan, and then it all came back, her lack of trust and Dan's anger. Instead, she telephoned Carolyn to ask who she knew that could come and clear the ice and snow from the roof.

Dan went to check on Crash. The puppy was playing happily with a piece of chewy when Dan came through the door. Opening the cage, Dan reached in and scratched the puppy's ears. Then he systematically checked him over and satisfied himself that the pup was coming along just fine.

Closing the cage, he walked back into his apartment and headed to the coffeepot now perked and ready. He poured a mug and sat gloomily at the table. He'd had a rotten night. Every time he started to drift off to sleep he'd remember Cindy's accusation. His mind had worked away like a hamster in a wheel, never coming to a stop, never giving him the answers he needed.

How could he envision a life with someone who mistrusted him? On the other hand, how could he live his life without Cindy? Where on earth could she have gotten the idea he'd had a holiday with Gina in Ottawa? Sure, he'd gone to Ottawa but not for a holiday. There had been a symposium going on there. A friend from New Zealand had telephoned a few days before the conference to say he would be attending it and could they meet. Cindy had still been away in Nova Scotia so Dan had decided on the spur of the moment to go, spend some time with his friend and take in the symposium since he had nothing to else to do. Gina had asked if she could go along for the ride as her sister lived there. He'd delivered her to her sister's and picked her up when it was time to come home. As he recalled, they'd had a very pleasant trip home, sharing what they had done and seen in the nation's capital. It had certainly helped to pass the time during the four-hour trip.

Just then, the telephone rang. Dan was surprised to hear Carolyn's voice. When she explained that Cindy had been wakened by water dripping on her bed and that Carolyn and David intended to go and see what they could do for her, Dan found himself unable to refuse joining them. Angry as he was with her, Dan couldn't resist the need to help her.

Cindy was outside walking around the house hitting the icicles with a broom when she heard the sound of a vehicle coming up the road. Cindy leaned against the deck railing, interested to see which tradeperson would show up. Much to her surprise, not one but two vehicles came up the drive. The first was Carolyn's van with ladders clamped on the top. Her heart did a major somersault when she realized that the next vehicle belonged to Dan.

Carolyn got out of her van and clattered up on to the deck. "Show me the leak."

Cindy felt dizzy with relief. He was actually here. Did that mean that he'd forgiven her? Or had Carolyn approached him and he'd felt unable to refuse?

Glancing back as she led Carolyn into the house, she saw David and Dan lifting the ladders off the van.

Surely, she thought, as she directed Carolyn upstairs, they didn't intend to climb up on the roof.

As Cindy showed Carolyn the location of the leak, she tried to apologize. "Carolyn. I didn't mean you were to come out and look after this. You guys have helped me enough lately."

"It's alright, Cindy. We've been to church and had lunch. The man who might have come is in bed with the flu so we decided we'd see what we can do. I just happened to be talking to Dan this morning and told him about your leak. He offered to help, too."

Cindy looked sharply at Carolyn when she said this. Was it true or was Carolyn just playing Cupid?

Carolyn finished checking out the roof from the inside and then headed back downstairs. "The first thing to do is to get the snow off the rest of this roof. We brought roof shovels with extension handles that should reach up quite high."

"Who's going to climb the ladders?" asked Cindy.

Carolyn grinned. "Dan and I. David and you can hold them still. We'll start with the section over your bedroom. The winds seem to have funneled around both sides of the house and piled the snow higher there than anywhere else."

Carolyn stopped in her tracks and asked innocently, "How did you like The Pines? Was the food as good as I said it was?"

Amused by Carolyn's sudden interest in the food, Cindy said, "It was quite excellent. We had a lovely leek and carrot soup with the slightest suggestion of fennel to start. Next, I had—"

Carolyn interrupted. "Forget the food. How did you and Dan get along?"

Cindy chose her words carefully. "We had a lovely time. It's such a great place. Has great atmosphere."

Then, she hurried up on the deck where the men had placed the ladders and were extending the handles on the roof shovels.

Carolyn wasn't fooled. Something was wrong. She'd just have to try to find out later. Then she headed to the van to get some small boards, a hammer, nails and a rope.

While Carolyn made a ledge on the deck with the boards against which to brace the ladders and then tied them to the deck railings for stability, Cindy watched Dan out of the corner of her eye. He'd acknowledged her with a cool nod when he'd first arrived and now stood across the deck talking to David.

Going over to David, Carolyn took a shovel from him and said, "Close your eyes, sweetheart, and hold the ladder. Dan and I will be down in a few minutes. Don't be surprised if snow falls on your heads. Try to dodge."

Cindy peeked over at David as Carolyn clambered up the ladder. He was gripping the ladder so tightly that she could see his fingers were white with strain while he watched his wife ascend. Cindy tested her own ladder and was convinced it was secure, then stood aside to let Dan climb up. He brushed closely by her, and in the warm clear air of the thaw, the scent of his aftershave tantalized her. Unfortunately, her nearness didn't seem to affect him a bit. Clasping the sides of the ladder, he clambered up without a glance. He stopped near the top of the ladder and started pulling down the snow.

For the next hour, the four of them worked, and in spite of her anxiety about Dan's attitude, Cindy found herself frequently laughing when snow clouded down and settled over her hair and down her neck. Satisfied at last that the roof was clear enough, the ladders and shovels were packed away.

Cindy and David made cocoa while Carolyn went up into the attic to see if she could repair the leak. Dan went along to hold the ladder. When they returned Carolyn said, "I think you'll be alright for now but you should phone your insurance company and see about getting the ceiling repaired. They may want your parents to get a new roof. Do you know how old it is?"

Cindy had only a vague memory of when it was last shingled. She shrugged. "Maybe ten years. I'll get in touch with my parents tomorrow morning. I was talking to them yesterday and they said they were going to visit friends today."

Glancing at her watch, Cindy saw that it was nearly four-thirty. Dan was still cool, not instigating conversation or looking at her unless he had to. She felt a burst of annoyance. Darn him, she thought. If the shoe had been on the other foot, he'd have probably been jealous too. She wasn't going to let him get away with this.

Inspiration hit. "I have an idea. If you are free tonight, why don't we have our Scrabble game. I made some meat sauce just the other day so we could have spaghetti and salad. I also baked bread. We can make garlic bread to go with it. Also," she paused, "it will give me a chance to express my appreciation."

Carolyn and David glanced at each other, then David said, "Sounds like a great idea."

Cindy looked at Dan for a long moment. Finally, he shrugged. "Sure, why not. That's if you'll wait a half an hour while I check on Crash, a cat and a sick pet rat."

* * *

Cindy hurried about setting the table while the sauce was warming. It smelled delicious. Carolyn and David were busy making the salad. When Dan returned, she would put the pasta in the boiling water. She wanted everything to look just right. Somehow, she had to find a way to make peace with him. All the same, a tiny flicker of rebellion was beginning to gain life in Cindy. This was their first argument. If he was going to go off in a huff every time they argued, they'd never manage over time.

At that moment, Dan knocked on the door and walked in. Tall, his fair hair obviously still damp from a shower, he looked good enough to eat. He had changed into a green sweater that picked up the color in his hazel eyes and fresh jeans. He handed her his jacket and when their hands touched, she felt it all the way to her toes but he stepped back and hurried into the kitchen to the others.

When David saw him, he said, "What are you doing, Dan? Trying to put me to shame?"

"After checking the animals, I thought it was only prudent to change."

David raised one eyebrow knowingly and said, "Yeah, I'm sure that's why."

Dan refused to bite and Cindy said hurriedly, "I'm putting the pasta in now. Supper will be in a very few minutes."

The food was good but Cindy couldn't exactly call the occasion a success. David and Dan did most of the talking while Carolyn sat listening, her eyes shifting back and forth between Dan and her. When they were finished, David announced, "I suggest that Cindy and Dan set up the Scrabble board while Carolyn and I do the dishes. We don't want Cindy using her hand any more than she has to."

Dan was about to argue, after all he'd enjoyed his meal very much and felt obliged to help clean up. Also, he was a little concerned that David was being a bit obvious about making sure he was with Cindy. But before he could object, Cindy said, "Actually, that's a good idea. I thought we'd play at the dining-room table as the light is good but I need help making the table smaller." Two very delighted Cupids busily cleared the table and did the dishes while the Scrabble game was set up.

Dan stood gravely by the table and asked, "How can I help?"

Cindy felt like saying, You could try smiling. However she restrained herself and told him how to take the board out of the table. That done, she held the table steady with her good hand while he pushed the parts together. Then she handed him a cover her mother had made to protect the table when the family were using it to play games. She left him to put it on while she got out the Scrabble board.

When the dishes were finished, David came in, rubbing his hands with enthusiasm and announced, "I love Scrabble."

Carolyn added glumly, "And he always wins."

"Not tonight," said Cindy, picking up a tile. "I love Scrabble too, and *I* always win."

After they had each picked a tile and discovered that David went first, they settled down to study their seven letters.

"I think you might just be in for a little surprise," said David. He picked up his tiles. "Let me introduce you to some really good Scrabble playing." They watched as he made 'compute' centered across the middle. "Double word and I used all my tiles. Beat that my dear Cindy." With a flourish, he wrote down his beginning score. Dan and Carolyn groaned and fiddled with their tiles.

Cindy studied the board then stared at her row of tiles. D A M R I Z E. The R-I-Z-E-D jumped out at her. It was all she could do not to show her excitement. If Dan didn't use the space, she'd get a triple word score at the side.

Dan took forever to place the tiles and ended up with 'raze' built on the 'c' in 'computer'. Then it was her turn. With a whoop of enthusiasm, Cindy added her letters and made 'computerized'. "Eat your heart out, you guys. That was a triple word score. Thank you, David."

Dan watching thought, this is the Cindy I love; eyes sparkling, her dimple dancing on her left cheek, her curls bouncing with enthusiasm. His heart ached. He hated to feel so betrayed by her, so angry.

The game continued. Several times, a word was challenged. Once, Carolyn was caught making up a word she claimed was used in wood-working. Then, Dan made the word 'trust'. "Important word, don't you think?" he asked, looking directly at Cindy.

David, ever interested in ideas, proceeded to lead the discussion on the importance of trust in government, business and relationships. It was only when Carolyn kicked him under the table that the game continued. Finally they were down to the last tiles and Cindy and David were tied. Then Cindy placed 'wysiwyg' on a triple letter and used up all her tiles.

Dan and Carolyn said together, "That's not a word."

David just sat there with his mouth hanging open. "How did you know that word?"

The others gaped at him. "It's a real word?" asked Dan.

"You betcha," said David. "It's an adjective. It

means, if I remember the Webster correctly, 'of or being a computer screen display that shows text exactly as it will appear when printed'. Check your dictionary if you don't believe me."

Carolyn was busy adding up the final scores. "She cleaned your deck, David darling. When are we going to have a play-off?"

"Well, not tonight," David replied. "Take a look at Dan."

The others immediately looked at Dan who was caught guiltily trying to cover a yawn.

At that moment, the telephone rang and Cindy answered it. No one paid much attention to the call. They assumed it was Cindy's parents checking in. Something in her stance caught Dan's attention and he started to listen.

Cindy was saying, "Don't worry about it, Mike. You must go and take the family with you. It's a wonderful opportunity. Just think, a year in England and all expenses paid. I bet they put you up at a first-class hotel in London for the holidays. . . . No, I'll be alright. . . . Positive." She turned away from them and he heard her add . . . "friends."

When she hung up the phone, her shoulders drooped for a moment, then straightening, she hurried back to the table where the others were tidying up the game.

Carolyn asked, "What was that about, Cindy?"

She answered casually, "Nothing."

"Who is going to England?" Dan asked, curious in spite of himself.

By now, all three sets of eyes were on her. Picking up the Scrabble box, she said as she headed for the cupboard in which it was stored, "My brother's company has given him a big promotion and is sending the entire family to England immediately."

So that's it, thought Dan. She's going to be alone at Christmas. Before he could figure out just how to ask, Carolyn said, "That means you'll be alone for Christmas."

Cindy had her back to them and shrugged.

"You can spend Christmas with us."

Cindy turned about to reject such an idea but Carolyn continued, "Look, everyone is coming to our house for Christmas. My brothers and their families and my dad and Dan, too."

Cindy looked at Dan, surprised. "It's true," he said. "My parents are in Vancouver with my sister this Christmas. They take turns between us. I had them last year."

"C'mon, Cindy. It will be fun. And," said David with a great big grin, "You can help cook. Boy oh boy. A gourmet Christmas."

"But it's your first Christmas together," Cindy pointed out.

"That's true," said Carolyn, "but our house is made for a large family. We want to have everyone we know and love with us to enjoy it. Please say you'll come."

She glanced at Dan who sat there with a disinterested look. Angry again, she decided that she wasn't going to spoil her Christmas just because he was being a jerk. "Put like that, I'll be happy to come."

As the Reids and Dan began to put on their coats to leave, Carolyn asked Cindy, "What are your plans for the next few days?"

"I'm going to start work on a new project. The last one didn't work out. Too complicated. Thanks to Dan, I have a new and better idea for my assignment."

Determined to stay in Dan's face and defy the distance he was trying to put between them, she turned to Dan and said, "If it's okay, I'll drop in to see your patient whenever I can."

"Fine," he shrugged. "I'll probably see you there. I'll be busy sorting Merry out. Otherwise, I'll see you on Wednesday when we paint the floats." Then, in spite of himself, he teased, "That's if we can keep you away from rusty nails. How is your hand?"

Cindy held it up. "It isn't hurting anymore. I just have to remember not to put it in water or do anything too complicated with it."

They all trooped out and Cindy shut the door. For a moment, she felt lonely and a little sorry for herself. It would be her first time away from her family at Christmas. Then she remembered that she would be at Carolyn and David's and that Dan would be there too. A little flutter of hope followed her up the stairs to bed.

The small seed of hope still remained the next morning. When Cindy woke and looked out the window at the sun on the newly exposed green grass that the early snow had protected from the deep frosts of winter, that small seed blossomed a little. With it came determination to try to overcome the chasm that had grown between herself and Dan and an equal determination to stand up for herself. The information Gina had given her had been very believable. Instead of going off indignantly accusing her of a lack of trust, Dan could have asked her why she could believe he might take up with Gina.

On the other hand, Cindy thought ruefully, neither of them had been too sensible. She admitted to herself that she'd been wrong in not defending herself instead of dissolving in a blob of tears. A good fight might have cleared the air.

As she dressed, Cindy decided she would concentrate on her project. Her dream was still fresh in her mind. She would use its details to get her started. Maybe all her dreams were possible.

After breakfast Cindy contacted her parents and then the insurance company about the roof. Finally, she settled down to do some serious thinking. Her mind had obviously been working overtime because the minute she picked up her pencil she was off. One of the first things she wanted to do was check the laws covering tearooms. Her instructor was always quick to point it out when a student hadn't properly researched his or her project.

Her first stop, then, was the small community library in Stewart's Falls. It was in an old limestone building complete with fireplace and slightly sloping floors but Cindy had always loved it. She waited until she caught the attention of a pleasant young woman at the desk. She was new to Cindy; not very tall and just a little plump, with light brown hair, blue eyes and a fantastic complexion. "Hi," Cindy said, "I believe I met you at the Reids' at their house-warming party. I'm Cindy Howard."

"I remember you," the librarian said.

She's British, Cindy thought when she heard her speak.

The librarian came to the counter. "You made all that wonderful food. I wish you were going to be around here later in the year when we have our open house. But I understand you are returning to college."

Pleased at the compliment, Cindy said, "I'm finished at the end of January. I'm not sure what I'm doing then."

"We could use someone like you when we have

special meetings and open houses. Why don't you think about setting up a business here?"

"It's something to think about," Cindy said and thought of the imaginary tearoom she was planning.

"By the way," the librarian continued, "I'm Margaret Henshaw. How can I help you?"

"I've come in to get some information for the final project for my course. The topic I've chosen is the establishment of a tearoom that will serve food between nine in the morning and five in the afternoon. I imagine this tearoom in an older home so I have to find out all the regulations that one would have to follow."

"You'd want to know about zoning," Margaret said. "You couldn't choose just any old house."

"I hadn't thought of that," said Cindy. "I also would have to have a look at the food handling regulations for such an establishment and the fire and safety regulations. I need to do this very quickly since I'll soon be running out of time."

Margaret looked around. Just then a volunteer came in and walked behind the counter. "Karen," Margaret said, "would you hold the fort while I help Cindy. If you run into any trouble, come and see me. I'll be at one of the computers."

Turning to Cindy, she said, "There are four computers in the back of the library. Lucky for us, two are connected to the Internet. You can work on one and I'll work on the other. I suggest you try to find the information you want about food and I'll try to check out zoning, fire and safety regulations."

An hour later, Cindy was relieved to discover that between the two of them, they'd found every regulation she could think of and printed them out. Packing up all the information, Cindy said, "Margaret, I can't thank you enough. You've saved me so much time."

"That's what I'm here for," Margaret said and headed for the reception counter.

Curious, Cindy asked, "How long have you been in Stewart's Falls?"

"I came in October when Mrs. Smythe retired."

Thinking of the group meeting on Wednesday, Cindy asked, "Have you made many friends yet?"

Margaret shook her head. "Not really. Being single, it's hard to meet people. All the volunteers are married or seniors. I really haven't made contact with many people my own age except the Reids. Carolyn is often in checking out references and David has taken to working with some gifted kids in mathematics on Monday after school."

Cindy thought that Margaret might be around twenty-eight. Certainly a good age to join the tennis club which in the winter became the badminton club. On impulse, Cindy said, "Why don't you come out on Wednesday and help us paint the floats that are being repaired for the Santa Claus parade this Saturday?"

Margaret brightened at that. "I'd love to. Where do I go and what time?"

"I'll pick you up at seven o'clock. Tell me where you live."

They exchanged addresses and Cindy went off with her pile of regulations. Before she went back to the lake, she dropped in to see Crash.

Dan was just lifting Crash out of his cage when Cindy walked through the door from the reception area. Overnight, he'd worked out that he had been upset with Cindy because she'd hurt his feelings and showed an appalling lack of faith. In spite of this, his spirits lifted when he saw her. She was wearing a heavy knit red sweater with her jeans and hiking boots. No jacket. "You must think it's spring."

"It sure feels like it. There's hardly any snow left. It suppose it would have been nice to have some for the Santa Claus Parade."

As soon as Crash saw her, he tried to get out of Dan's arms. "It looks like he's feeling a lot better," said Cindy.

"He's growing like a weed. I'm just going to check the splint on his leg. Why don't you come into the examining room and hold him still while I do it."

She glowed with pleasure at the request. "I'd love to."

Dan led the way to one of the rooms. Carefully, he set the wriggling puppy on the metal examining table. "You need to keep him sitting on his haunches as I check his leg. He still shouldn't be moving too much because of the other injury."

Putting his hand on the puppy's haunches, he encouraged him to sit down. Cindy placed her hand where Dan's was and kept her other hand under Crash's chest. All the while the puppy's tail was swishing back and forth with delight at seeing her. She leaned over, crooning to him while he licked her face. Cindy giggled and talked nonsense while Dan checked the leg.

"I think we can leave that splint on for another day or so. That's the second one he's had."

"He's growing that fast?" asked Cindy.

"Yes, but that's not the only reason I changed the splint. He's only a puppy and he hasn't been trained, nor has he been in any condition to be trained. His splint gets soiled."

Cindy suddenly felt overcome with remorse. Dan

was so busy and here he was worrying about this pup. Reaching over, she tentatively touched his hand. "Dan, I'm so sorry I've added to your work load."

Dan was surprised. "I told you I was happy to do it. We made a bargain. You cater for me and I'll care for Crash. Anyway, Merry is here now to ease the pressure. She's in one of the other examining rooms meeting Augustus, our very toughest customer."

At that point they heard the sound of feline disgust rise to a screech.

"Do you think she needs some help?" asked Cindy.

Dan shook his head. "Merry's a pro. She'll soon have Augustus eating out of her hand. He loves his food. He'll do anything for cat candies."

Cindy laughed. "You mean you actually bribe your patients?"

"You do what you have to do. Come on. You can carry Crash. I'm going to put him in a larger cage so he can get some exercise. Then, I'll introduce you to Augustus."

While they'd been checking the splint, a technician had prepared a fresh cage for Crash. The puppy wasn't too happy when Cindy put him in his cage but once he found a toy to chew on, he settled quite happily.

Touching Cindy on the shoulder, he nodded his head toward one of the other rooms. "Come and meet Augustus. He's a sight to behold."

Tapping on the door, they waited until Merry called, "Come in."

Dan entered with Cindy behind. "Augustus," Dan announced. On the table stuffing his face with cat candies was the biggest brown tabby she'd ever seen. At their entrance, he turned wicked yellow eyes at them and growled, then continued to chomp on the food.

"Did you think I was killing him?" asked Merry, winking at the older gentleman standing by the table.

"It sounded more like he was killing you," said Dan. "But we all know Augustus's weak spot, don't we, George. Especially as he's been on a diet."

The older gentleman laughed. "I think after today, when I show him the cage, instead of disappearing he'll leap into it. Eating diet food has not made him the happiest cat in the world."

Merry grinned. "I bet you have to watch your supper, George."

"He's taken to sitting beside me and reaching out with his paw for the plate. He's not happy when he's discouraged. He has quite a vocabulary of swear words."

Merry expertly gave Augustus his last shot while he still had a crunchy in his mouth. She tossed one into the cage and Augustus followed. George quickly locked the door and Augustus snarled.

"He's really quite a pleasant cat at home," George said. They all laughed.

As Cindy went to leave the clinic Dan asked, "How's your day gone so far?"

"Really well. I talked to my parents and the insurance agent. They're going to send out an adjuster right away to look at the damage."

"And your project?" asked Dan.

"I spent the rest of the time at the library. The new librarian is terrific. I have a mountain of material she helped me get off the Internet. All the regulations I'll need to know for a tearoom. I'm going to start work on them as soon as I've had lunch."

Dan was about to suggest she have lunch when Gina stuck her head through the reception room doors and said, "Dan. Floyd Junkin needs to talk to you. It's an emergency."

As Gina disappeared through the doors again, Cindy couldn't help but glower. Glancing at Dan, she saw that he was watching her. Not feeling ready to confront him, she said, "I'll see you Wednesday."

To her surprise, he said, "I'll pick you up," as he headed for the phone. "Six forty-five."

So, Cindy thought as she headed outside to her car, we're speaking and he's picking me up. That's a start.

Dan picked Cindy up at six forty-five on the dot. On the way to the librarian's home Dan said, "I'm glad you invited Margaret. She's new in town. When she first came, she was very busy getting settled. As a result, I think she missed out on the autumn activities."

"She was a great help to me," said Cindy. "She saved me a tremendous amount of time."

"Then, we'd better make sure she has a really good time tonight. By the way," he added, "I find myself looking at all the older houses in town to see if they'd be suitable for a tearoom. I figured if I could spot a house, you could look at it, maybe even take a picture of it and use it as a sample model."

Cindy was touched by this. It sounded almost as if Dan wanted her to have a tearoom in Stewart's Falls. He certainly seemed keen to help her. "Well," she said, "if you do see one, keep in mind that it will have to be in a commercially zoned area."

"I hadn't thought of that," he said as he drove up to Margaret's flat on the bottom floor of a Victorian mansion. "How would a place like this be?"

Cindy looked at it critically for a moment, then said, "I think it would be too big, don't you? Too many rooms." Opening the door, she said, "I'll just run in and get Margaret."

Once they'd picked up Margaret they headed for the lumber yard and joined the others who were all crowded around the float containing Santa's sled and the descending reindeer. When Carolyn was sure everyone was present, she said, "Thanks to David and Dan we are going to have the most wonderful float. The other villages will eat their hearts out. Let me demonstrate.

"We chose to use a battery as our source of energy, thanks to Andy's expertise." She nodded toward her tall shy brother who sang of broken hearts. She turned a switch and immediately several things happened. Rudolph's nose lit up a bright red and the reindeer appeared to be landing gently on the float.

"That's fantastic," someone said to Carolyn.

"Thank my genius husband for the idea," she said. David laughed and bowed with a flourish.

"Now," Carolyn continued, "Henry here is going to help you make these poor cut-out reindeer come to life by showing you all how to paint them."

Henry, the high-school art teacher, stepped forward and assigned them all jobs. The least confident were given the job of painting a foundation coat on each of the reindeer. Several of the more experienced workers were given the job of working on the other float, painting the church which was now a three-dimensional structure rather than the flat outline Dan and Cindy had taken apart. Carolyn had also constructed two houses, very thin but wide enough to allow someone to be inside the front doors ready to greet the carollers. A path led from each house to the church and around behind the houses so the singers could walk along the float as they sang.

Margaret and Cindy each worked on a reindeer while Dan went off to help David. Very soon, all the people painting reindeer were making themselves known to Margaret. Cindy could see that she was having a really good time.

Cindy finished her reindeer and looked around for Henry for another job when she saw Gina saunter in. She waved to some of the group who were working on the other float. When she noticed Dan, she took off her coat and headed in his direction. Cindy looked at her paint can and thought, I'd like to pour paint all over her. Then she was ashamed of herself and a little shaken by the strength of her jealousy.

Carolyn looked up in time to notice Cindy's expression and checked to see what had upset her. She saw Gina beside Dan and all her Cupid instincts took over. In a flash she was over beside Gina saying, "Gina, I'm so glad you could come. I have just the job for you." She led her to a number of strings of Christmas tree lights. "These need to be checked. There's a plug on the wall over by the other float. Why don't you take that old crate to sit on and do it over there."

With a pained expression on her face, Gina picked up the lights and did as she was bid. For a moment, Carolyn felt guilty. Sorting those little lights was a lousy job. When she noticed the look of relief on Cindy's face she grinned smugly. After all, a Cupid had to do what a Cupid had to do.

Cindy smiled smugly too and then felt ashamed of herself. Turning to Henry, she said, "I think that paint is dry enough for me to move on to step two." Margaret looked up and said, "I'm ready, too."

"Which of you has had some experience painting anything besides flat surfaces?"

Margaret, with her soft cultured voice, answered, "I do watercolors."

Cindy watched with fascination as Henry, the most solid of individuals, lit up with delight. "Margaret," and then with a twinkle, "Maggie, you paint?"

"Yes. I just haven't had time to get back at it since I've moved here but I intend to do so, soon."

Henry said diffidently, "Maybe we could paint together sometime. I do watercolors also."

Now Margaret colored delightfully. "I'd enjoy that." Then realizing that Cindy was watching them with interest, Margaret said, "What do you want us to do now?"

Turning to Cindy, Henry said, "I'd like you to put shading on the reindeer to make them appear three dimensional. I'll show you how and then you can show the rest of the painters as they finish with the undercoat. Maggie, if you'll wait a moment, I'll show you how I'd like the eyes done."

Henry had just started teaching at the local high school when Cindy was in her second to last year. She knew the art students liked him. Now, she found out one of the reasons. Patiently, he demonstrated what he wanted and then encouraged her to imitate him. Once they'd worked for a few minutes, he had her stand back a ways and told her look at her handiwork. She was amazed. The reindeer's stomach looked rounded.

He quickly showed her how to work around the neck and haunches of the animals and then left her to it.

"Come over here, Maggie," he instructed, and led her over to where two saw-horses held a plank of plywood. Taking up a scribbler, he showed Margaret how he wanted the eyes done. Cindy grinned and looked over at Carolyn who, with Cupid sensitivity, had been watching what was happening. Carolyn winked.

Just then, Dan spoke up behind her. Startled, she turned and looked at him. "How's the painting coming?" he asked.

Proudly, she showed him how she was adding depth to the wooden figures. Standing back, he squinted his eyes and said, "That's really good."

David came by and overheard Dan's remark. "Henry's a good teacher. He taught me to paint a tree last summer." He paused, then added, "With leaves."

When Dan and Cindy looked at him blankly, he explained, "I'd never painted anything in my life before. At least, if I did, I don't remember. Never was interested before."

Cindy remembered hearing that David was a bit of a genius. She knew he'd made his fortune in the field of electronics. She also knew that now he did some teaching at a nearby university an hour's drive away. It hadn't crossed her mind before that someone so very gifted might not spend his time at the things other kids dabbled in as they were growing up.

Finally, all the reindeer were painted, shaped and had large, eloquent eyes applied by Maggie and Henry.

As they packed up, Carolyn said to them all, "I hope some of you can help tomorrow night. I think we'll just finish in time for the rehearsal on Friday night."

Dan indicated that he could come but Cindy hesitated. She really had to work on her assignment. When it came time to go home, Margaret came up with Henry and blushing prettily said, "Henry said he'd take me home if that's okay with you."

Dan assured her that he didn't mind and hummed

all the way to his SUV. The minute they were inside it, he said, "Did you see that? I think Henry's smitten."

Cindy agreed. "I think it's terrific. He's such a nice person." Then thinking about Margaret, she said, "I bet she'd never been called Maggie before. She loved it."

Dan drove down the main street through town. When they stopped at the only traffic light, Cindy suddenly pointed. "Look, Dan. There's a puppy. Just like Crash."

Dan followed her finger and sure enough, there was a puppy tearing away at a bag of garbage set out in front of the coffee shop. Pulling over, he said, "Let's see if we can catch it."

They got out quietly and approached the animal cautiously. They were less than a store length away when it looked up and saw them. It took off immediately. They tried to follow but it wiggled between the drug store and another building placed so closely together that they were unable to squeeze through.

"There's no point in going after it now," Dan said. "It'll be hiding. Phil told me that there's some kind of heating duct in there where the puppy keeps warm. He's been leaving food out for it. He's hoping to tame it and bring it in."

Cindy looked at him, worried about what 'brought in' might mean. Dan noticed her expression and said, "Don't worry. If it's caught, I'll try to find a home for it. The problem is that the pup will have trouble when the temperature really dives and it gets too big to get between the buildings."

As they headed out of town toward the lake, Cindy asked how things were going with Merry. "She's doing fine. I would have suggested she come tonight but I knew that she was tired. I understand she talked to your parents. When is she coming over to see the house?"

"I suggested she come over tomorrow on her lunch hour, if that can be arranged. It would be best to see it in the daylight."

"I'll make sure she's free. By the way, what did the insurance company say?"

"They're sending out an adjuster tomorrow at ten. When he's decided what's to be done, he'll talk to my parents."

They turned in the lake road and twisted along between the evergreens that grew by the roadside. "I wish the snow hadn't melted," said Cindy. "I love winter." Then she qualified that. "At least, I like it when it's cold and there is proper snow on the ground and ice on the lake."

"I'm sure you'll get your wish," Dan said dryly.

Cindy glanced over at him. He hadn't said much since leaving the town. Maybe he's worrying about the pup, she thought.

Dan was worrying, but not about the puppy. He knew he should clear things up with Cindy, tell her she'd hurt him with her accusations and try to find out where she'd got this such a ridiculous notion about Gina. But his feelings were still too raw.

When they reached the house, Cindy hopped out before he could get his door opened, leaned in and said, "Thanks for the ride, Dan. Maybe I'll see you tomorrow night. I really have to work hard tomorrow. If I get enough done, I'll go."

She shut the SUV's door, ran up the path to the house and unlocked the door. Waving a hand, she disappeared inside.

Dan sighed. He had a feeling Cindy was just as cautious as he was about discussing their problem.

Chapter Five

Dan stopped in front of a two-story house set back on a corner lot. He had always liked this house. It had an attractive entrance with glass door-panels and a fan window above the entrance. Off the side of the house was a large sunroom, no doubt added some years after the house was built.

His visit today was not a happy one. Alice Thornton, his client, was a pretty grey-haired woman in her mid-seventies. She was always dressed as if she was just going out; pretty blouses, neat skirts or trousers and polished shoes on her tiny feet. She had the bluest eyes he'd ever seen; eyes that always twinkled with mischief. She was a tease, always wanting to know when he intended to settle down and find a nice village girl. Little did she know that he'd tried and his efforts had blown up in his face.

But today, there would be no teasing. Alice was recovering from a broken hip and Dan had a horrible feeling that her beloved Sweet Pea, the sweetest calico cat he'd ever seen, might be the reason she asked him to come.

Dan got out of the car and walked up on the verandah. Knocking at the door, he waited and listened. In a moment, he heard a soft shuffle of feet and then the door opened and Alice's head appeared around it. "Come in, dear," she said in a thready voice, so unlike her usually clear tones.

Leaning on a walker, she backed up enough for him to slip in the door. "You'll have to hang your coat up for me," she said. "I hope you'll stay for a cup of tea. My daughter left it ready for us in the sun room."

Dan had expected this invitation. He'd had tea twice with Alice over the past year when Sweet Pea needed attention, although Dan suspected that part of the reason for those visits was that Alice was lonely and had nothing to do but worry about Sweet Pea, the healthiest young cat on his patient list.

Dan followed Alice through the living room into the large sunroom. It was a pleasant room with a TV, a sofa and chair, and a coffee table on which sat a delicate china tea set; teapot, cream and sugar and two elegant teacups. The teapot was tucked snugly into a pink crocheted tea cosy. The waiting plate of brownies made Dan's mouth water.

He helped Alice into a chair and was about to sit down when he heard a familiar chrr. Seconds later, the small calico settled in Alice's lap. With trembling hands she stroked the cat for a moment, and then said, "Would you pour, dear, my hands aren't very steady yet. I've only been home from the hospital for a week."

"You're doing very well," observed Dan. "You'll be doing wheelies with that walker before long."

"Not soon enough," she smiled sadly. "The doctors made it clear that I should no longer be living in this house by myself. My daughter found me an apartment in the new senior's complex that just opened. I can work in my own kitchen or take meals in a dining room. Several of my friends are already there so we can have a game of bridge or gossip whenever we want. It is really very nice. I can even take quite a lot of my furniture."

Dan poured milk into a tea cup, added the tea and half a teaspoon of sugar and handed it to her.

"You've remembered how I like it." Then with a twinkle of her old self, she added, "You'll make someone a wonderful husband some day."

"Now Alice," he grinned. "Stop teasing and drink your tea."

Dan poured himself a cup of tea and added the milk after. He did it this way to make her smile. They always argued which was the best time to put milk in the tea.

For a while they sipped their tea and Dan consumed brownies. As usual, they were delicious and he said so. Alice explained, "My daughter made them. She uses my recipe. Has for years. Her kids love them."

Finally, they came to the hard part of the afternoon. "Dan, I have a favor to ask of you. I know it isn't a fair thing to ask but I'm going to ask anyway."

As if knowing what was to come next, Sweet Pea slipped off her mistress's lap and leaped lightly onto the back of his chair. She began to tickle his neck and jaw with her whiskers while purring loudly. Putting down his tea cup, Dan lifted the cat down onto his lap. "You're a shameless flirt, Sweet Pea." Having arrived where she wished to be, Sweet Pea yawned, circled and settled down.

Alice's voice trembled. "I think she knows what I'm going to say. You see, they don't think I should take Sweet Pea with me. After all, she was the reason I fell and broke my hip. I tripped over her."

Dan hadn't known that.

"I know I'm asking a lot but I wondered if you could find a new home for Sweet Pea. She's young enough to adapt. She loves children. You've seen her play with my neighbors' kids." Her eyes teared up in spite of herself. "She's too full of life to be put down."

At that, Sweet Pea opened her eyes, rolled on her back and shamelessly licked Dan's fingers.

Alice continued. "My daughter would take her but my granddaughter has asthma and being near the cat triggers an attack."

If anything, Dan felt relief. He'd been afraid she was going to ask him to put Sweet Pea down thinking that it would be kinder than leaving her behind. He knew it would have broken her heart. He wasn't sure how he was going to find a home for a three-year-old cat, not even one as clever as Sweet Pea. People always wanted kittens. But he'd look after her.

"When are you moving, Alice?"

"Next Monday. My daughter is helping me decide what to bring. She's also going to go through things and take anything she wants. After that, the house will be sold and the contents disposed of."

"Well, why don't you keep Sweet Pea until Sunday. I'll come by then and pick her up. I'm sure I'll find her a home. Don't worry. I won't put her down."

"I know I'm just a silly old woman," she said, "worrying about a cat. But Sweet Pea is special. She's been my companion ever since my husband died."

They talked a little while longer about her new apartment and what things she might take with her.

While they talked, Dan became aware that he was looking around the sun porch as if he'd never seen it before. Suddenly, it clicked. This was the kind of place Cindy was talking about.

Leaning forward, he said, "Alice, I have a friend who is studying to be a chef. Cindy Howard. You probably know her parents. They owned the drug store in town until a few years ago when he retired and sold out."

"Of course I know Cindy."

"Well," Dan explained, "Cindy is doing a major project to finish her cooking course next month. She's pretending she's opening a tearoom. She imagined a house something like yours in which to put her tea room. Would you consider letting her come and see it? Maybe even take some pictures to include in her assignment?"

"Cindy is special to you?" asked Alice.

"Yes." And suddenly, Dan knew that he meant that with all his heart.

Alice was from a long line of Cupids and even at seventy-five, her wings could flutter at an opportunity to do a little matchmaking. "I'd love to see Cindy again and let her take pictures or measurements or anything else she wants to do. But she'd better do it soon. Do you think she could come early tomorrow, around ten o'clock, before we start tearing everything apart?"

"I'm sure she'll come at ten tomorrow. I'll let you know at supper time if she can't. She'll probably phone you herself."

Well pleased with this suggestion, Dan said good-bye to Alice and headed out to Cindy's.

* * *

As Cindy set the table she reviewed her morning. Up early, she had worked hard until ten when the appraiser arrived. He was there for almost three-quarters of an hour with a contractor. The two men checked the roof, the attic and the bedroom ceiling. They talked to her parents in Florida, made arrangements to start the repair work and then departed.

Cindy had been relieved that they felt a little work inside the attic would avoid any other leaks as long as the roof was cleared after heavy falls of snow. A date was set for the contractor to come out and start the repairs to the bedroom.

After they left, Cindy quickly made a small quiche suitable for two, put it in the oven and then squeezed in another half hour's work on her project. She just had time to throw together a salad and butter some rolls to be heated in the microwave when she heard Merry drive up.

Merry rushed in, sure she was late. She was dressed casually in jeans and shirt and brought along loafers in which to slip her feet. "You could have worn your runners," said Cindy. "It's just like an autumn day outside."

"You wouldn't want my runners in your house. Goodness knows what might be on them. I spent part of the time in a barn with a very cautious farmer who wasn't convinced that I knew anything about dairy cattle. Once I told him I'd been brought up on a dairy farm, he settled down."

Cindy led Merry to a chair by the fireplace. "Give me a minute to get the food out and we can eat. Would you prefer tea or coffee?"

"Coffee," said Merry and leaned back and closed her eyes. "It's great to relax. I've found these first days nerve-wracking. It will be better when I get to know people."

Cindy was startled at that. Merry sounded a little shy. She seemed so positive in her manner that it was hard to imagine.

When the food was ready, Merry joined Cindy at the table. "Mmmm. Everything smells delicious. Dan tells me that you're training to be a chef."

Cindy nodded. "I will be qualified by the end of January if the project I'm working on is accepted and I pass the exams."

They ate for a few minutes, enjoying each other's company and discussing the coming Santa Claus Parade. It wasn't until Cindy asked Merry about her little boy that the conversation became more serious. "He's four and should be ready to start kindergarten next September," said Merry. "That's why I want to get settled as soon as possible. I've been enquiring and there is a junior kindergarten he can go to right now but I'll have to find a suitable person to look after him for the part of the day he's not at school."

"I'll ask around," said Cindy. "I'll ask tonight if I make it to work on the Christmas floats. Dan is definitely going tonight. Ask him to mention it."

"Dan told me about the broken floats. He said you'd hurt your hand. How is it?"

Cindy held it up and looked at the bandage. "It really seems to be fine. The stitches come out in a few days."

Merry grinned. "I heard about the stitches. Seems that Dan passed out."

Cindy was surprised. "He told you about it?"

"A client was kidding him. It was too good a story not to get passed around. I gather you were the cause."

"Me?"

"Dan said he saw that needle coming near your hand and it was game over."

Cindy blushed.

Merry said, "I think you must be special to Dan."

Cindy blushed again and got up to serve the coffee and some cookies.

When she returned, Merry said, "Now tell me about the house and then I'd better take a look at it and get back to work. Just sitting here, I can tell I would love to live in it."

When they finished their coffee, Cindy took her on a tour. She suggested that Merry use her bedroom with its ensuite washroom if the repairs were finished by then. If not, there was another guest room. Cindy also showed her her brother's old bedroom suitably decorated for a boy. In the end, it only needed Merry to call her parents and settle the matter.

When Merry left, Cindy settled back to work. It wasn't until she heard a car drive up as darkness began to fall that she realized how late it was. Going to the window, she was surprised to see Dan climbing up on the deck. She waved and let him in.

Cindy's heart began to pound. Had the moment come when they had to discuss their problem? Had Dan come for an explanation? Could she justify the one she had? Opening the door, she greeted him with a very cautious "Hi," and let him in.

He glanced at the books on the dining-room table. "I hope I'm not disturbing you. I thought you'd probably be taking a break by now."

Still not sure why he was there, Cindy said, "Give me your jacket. I've done as much as I can on the preliminary work. I'm going to start to plan the menus I'll serve after supper." Then deciding to take a risk because she was glad to see him, she said, "You're welcome to stay for supper if you like. Nothing special."

When he'd dropped by, it was merely to tell Cindy about Alice's house. The last thing he'd expected was an invitation to supper. Did she want to explain herself? Would her explanation be enough?

"I'd like to stay if it's not too much trouble. I know you're really busy with the project. Tell me what to do and I'll help."

Soon she had him scraping carrots, slicing onions and cutting up broccoli while she prepared chicken to stir fry. As they worked, he said, "I came over for a special reason."

Cindy's spirits plummeted. She wasn't ready for this.

Nervously, she joked, "Not to eat my cooking?"

"To be honest, I didn't think I'd be that lucky. To eat the cooking, that is. Anyway, I have something exciting to tell you. I've discovered the house for your tearoom project. If you're free tomorrow just before ten, I've made arrangements for you to see it. The owner is moving out on Monday. They are starting to pack tomorrow morning. She said they'd wait until you see it before they begin if you are interested."

Cindy was surprised at his enthusiasm and the kernel of hope she carried around flourished a little more. "I'd love to see the house. Tell me about it."

"It's over at the corner of Colborne and Newton Street. It was probably built in the 1920s. It has a winterized sun porch with a lovely view over the side yard. The living room even has a fireplace."

Cindy tried to imagine the corner. Suddenly she said, "Do you mean Mrs. Thornton's house?"

"Yes. I didn't realize you knew her," said Dan.

"Actually," Cindy explained. "My parents know her better than I do. I know her to speak to."

"She fell and broke her hip. She's able to make do with a walker now but has to move. She's going into one of those new apartments in the seniors' complex on the other side of town."

Cindy was sorry to hear that Alice had to leave her home. "You're sure she won't mind if I come over?"

"She knew you when I mentioned your name. She was happy to have you come. You're welcome to bring a camera and a tape measure, too."

"How come you were at Alice's today?"

Dan handed Cindy the washed and cut-up vegetables and said, "Actually, it's a very sad occasion. Alice has this delightful little calico cat. She can't take Sweet Pea with her. The cat is the reason she tripped and broke her hip. She asked me to find a good home and I said I would. Normally, I wouldn't make such a promise because it's not always possible. But for Alice, I didn't have the heart to say no. If I can't find a home, I guess I'll keep her myself."

"You really are a softie. First Crash and now Sweet Pea."

She was completely irresistible at that moment with her cheeks rosy from cooking, a soft smile on her lips and such a tender look in her eyes. Dan thought about taking her into his arms and kissing all their misunderstandings away. But even as the thought crossed his mind, she turned back to the stove and began to stir-fry the vegetables.

She pointed toward a buffet in the dining room. "You'll find placemats in the buffet. The stainless steel is in this drawer and the dishes in the cupboard below. By the time you have the table set, this will be ready."

As they ate, Dan learned all about food regulations

and zoning. At the end of the meal, Cindy said with disgust, "I'm really sorry. All I've talked about are dry rules and regulations. You're a sport to seem so interested."

Dan stood up and got the coffee pot. Pouring some into each of their mugs, he said, "I found it very interesting." Glancing at his watch, he said, "Look at the time. I gather from what you've said that you can't come tonight. I promised I'd be at the lumber yard by six-thirty. I'm sorry to leave you with the clean-up but I've got to go."

Gulping his coffee down, he said, "I'll pick you up at nine forty-five to see Alice." When she looked like she might object, he said, "I'd also like to be sure she's alright. She was pretty fragile yesterday. Anyway, I'm interested to see what you think of the house."

As he was heading out the door, Cindy remembered Merry's problem. "Merry needs to find to find someone to care for her little boy. Could you ask around tonight to see if anyone can think of someone suitable?"

"Sure. I should have thought of this myself. Thanks again for supper." With that, he headed out the door.

Cindy was ready the next morning when Dan drove up, wearing only a heavy cream sweater and jeans. It was sunny and definitely balmy for the fourteenth of December. Hopping into the car, she asked, "Do you figure we missed winter completely and passed through some time warp to April?"

"I'm not complaining. Makes my life a lot easier not to be risking life and limb through snow storms and over icy roads. Did you get a lot of work done last night?"

"Actually, I did. Completed the winter menu first

since I know what's available in the stores in town right now. I also know what food I'd have to get in Smithboro. It has much larger stores."

It wasn't far to Alice's and as they approached her street, Cindy felt a sense of growing anticipation. The houses were of the vintage she had imagined. When they drew up in front of Alice's house she knew it was perfect. It was as if the house she had imagined had been this house all the time. The sun porch extended off the side of what must be the living room so that it had a view of both streets. There was a large maple and an oak tree that would offer shade in the summer.

Dan led the way up the verandah steps and knocked. The door was answered by Alice's daughter. Cindy recognized her and remembered her name. "Hi, Karen. It was really good of your mom and you to let me see the house."

"I think it's good for Mom. It's distracting her from the upset of packing. I've started upstairs so you can see the downstairs undisturbed." Turning to Dan, she said, "I can't thank you enough for looking after Sweet Pea, Dr. Hamilton."

"Call me Dan. Your mom and I are old pals. I'm glad to do it for her. I've known that little rascal Sweet Pea ever since your mom got her."

After their coats had been disposed of, Karen led them into the living room where Alice was sitting at a card table wrapping knickknacks up in newspaper. When she started to rise, Cindy said, "Mrs. Thornton, please don't get up." Pulling up a chair, Cindy sat down across from her. "Thank you so much for letting me look at your house at such an awkward time. It is really going to make my project so much better, especially if I can take some pictures, too."

Alice sparkled at that. "I'm delighted, Cindy. I think my house will make a wonderful tea room."

"Oh, but . . ." Cindy was about to correct her when Dan said, "Where's Sweet Pea?"

Alice looked around. "She was here a moment ago, playing with a bit of newspaper that fell on the floor."

At that moment, something lit on Cindy's shoulder. Guessing right away that Sweet Pea had made an appearance, Cindy put her hand up just as she felt a cold nose in her ear and whiskers tickling her cheek. Laughing, Cindy lifted the cat down, settled her on her lap and began scratching her behind her ears. Sweet Pea purred in ecstacy.

Alice said, "Dan's going to look after her until he can find a home for her." Then looking at him, she said, "Do you think you could take her today, Dan? She has almost slipped outside twice. I'm afraid if she got out she would get lost. Some friends of Karen's are coming over to help after lunch. In the confusion, Sweet Peas might get in trouble."

Quite charmed by the young cat, Cindy said, "I could take Sweet Pea and keep her with me at the house until I go back to school. She'd be company for me. You'll probably find a home for her by then."

Alice just beamed. "You wouldn't mind? I'd be so relieved."

"That's settled, then. After I've looked around and made notes, I'll get Sweet Pea's things and the carrier and take her with me."

Picking up a clipboard she'd brought with her and getting her camera out of her purse, Cindy said, "I'd better get to work. I know Dan has to be back to the clinic soon."

Dan sat down where Cindy had been. "You look

around and I'll visit with Alice. If you need me to help you measure, just yell."

From the moment Cindy had walked in the door, she'd known that this house was the ideal location. The entrance was tiled and large enough to make it easy for a group of people to come in all at once. The woodwork in the house was oak as was the hardwood floor.

Cindy walked about the living room and sunroom. They were the perfect size. It was unnerving, as if a dream she'd had suddenly materialized. There was even a fireplace at the back of the living room with an oak mantle. Large windows in both rooms would let the light in during the winter while the trees would shade the rooms in the summer.

She wandered back into the hall and looked into the dining room. It would be a perfect room for a gift shop or, she thought, with a sudden flash of inspiration, a room that could be used for small catered events.

Down the hall was a washroom under the stairs. She supposed it had been put in for Alice's convenience. Beyond that was the kitchen. The room was large, running behind the dining room and hall. From the look of it, it had been modernized sometime in the last twenty years. It even had a washer and dryer in one corner, probably put there so Alice would not have to go down to the basement. Upstairs, Cindy found three bedrooms and a bathroom.

Taking out her book, Cindy began to sketch and measure room sizes, windows and doors. Then she took pictures. She finished by taking a picture of Alice with Sweet Pea on her lap and Dan standing by her chair.

Thanking Alice for letting her see the house, Cindy went to find Karen and get Sweet Pea's carrier, food and toys. Dan joined her as they collected the items. He said, "Cindy. You're sure it's alright if Sweet Pea goes with you? Your parents won't mind?"

"No, we've always had pets. It's the least I could do for Alice and for you. You'll have your hands full with Crash."

"Speaking of Crash," Dan said, "how would you like to help me replace his splint when we're finished here? The technicians are busy all day with other duties and that splint needs to be changed."

Dan held his breath while Cindy obviously thought through the things she had to do. Trying to tip the balance in his favor, he said, "I can order a pizza just before we leave here. When we arrive at the clinic, I'll give Crash a sedative. As it's taking effect, we can eat the pizza. We should have everything done by one o'clock and then, I'll take you home. How about it?"

Cindy looked to where Sweet Pea was helping Alice by jumping into a bag of newspapers by her chair. "What about Sweet Pea?"

"She'll be fine in her carrier for that short while. If she gets restless, maybe Gina will play with her. She likes cats."

Crash was very relaxed when Dan lifted him from his cage and placed him on the examining table. "Here, Cindy," Dan said, "place your hands on his shoulder to keep him steady." Taking a blunt pair of scissors, Dan began to cut through the tape, gauze and padding along the elbow and down the leg until the splint was slit on two sides.

"Now comes the tricky bit," he said. "You see, when the leg begins to knit, it develops something called 'callous'. It would be very easy to break this so I must work very carefully."

Cindy watched, fascinated, as Dan gently began to work the tape free that was attached to the puppy's fur that acted as an anchor. It took considerable time to do this and all the time, the puppy stayed fairly quiet.

Carefully he lifted the leg and cleaned it. When it was dry, he ran long runners of tape face down along the leg so that they projected well beyond either end.

"I have to extend the tape so that when we put the leg in the splint I can flip the ends back, and they will help hold the splint in place. Hopefully that will keep Crash from working the splint loose."

Dan had Cindy come around the table and, still keeping one hand on the puppy, with her other hand, slip a larger splint under the puppy's leg when Dan lifted it. The puppy let out a little whine and then settled back down.

Speaking quietly, Dan said, "Now try to keep the leg just where it is while I make sure the padding is correctly placed to prevent pressure sores." When that was done, he put the top half of the splint on and began to wind gauze around the splint and finally tape it securely. He took the extended ends that were actually stuck to the puppy's fur inside the splint and drew them back over the splint.

"There," he said. "That should hold it." Smiling at Cindy, he said, "Thanks, you were a great help." Cindy went to withdraw her hand from under the splint and their fingers touched. As if frozen, the two of them looked at each other, each wanting to say the right thing, to continue the touching, to find their place together again when there was a tap at the door and Mel, the young technician, hurried in. "I'm free to help now," he said.

With the greatest of care, each retrieved their fingers

and let the puppy's leg rest. If any of the village Cupids had been present, they would have knocked their two heads together and slammed the door on the face of the innocent technician. But unaware of how near their lovers had been to patching up their differences, they were unable to interfere.

Leaving Mel the technician to place Crash back in his larger cage, Cindy and Dan retreated to the reception area where Sweet Pea was entertaining Gina. Cindy watched for a few minutes. It was obvious that Gina liked playing with the cat. She was gentle with it and inventive in thinking of ways to amuse it. No wonder Dan depended on her. She was made for the job.

Cindy knew she could blow Gina's stories right up in her face at that very moment but in doing so, Dan would probably fire her and lose an excellent receptionist. There had to be a better way. The reception desk was no place for a confrontation. It was with some satisfaction that Cindy picked up Sweet Pea, thus ending the game.

Still thinking very dark thoughts about Mel the technician, Dan watched her while she did this. "Wait," he said. "You might as well have some food for Sweet Pea." Picking up a large bag of dry food, he said, "I think this would be best. Do you have any litter or a container for it?" By the time they headed out to his van to take her home, Cindy had enough supplies to keep the cat for weeks.

Having calmed down from the near-miss of whatever might have happened in the examining room, Cindy was able to tease, "You'll never get rich if you give all your products away."

Placing the food in the van, Dan said, "Believe me, the fact that you're caring for Sweet Pea makes any expense worth it. She is far too sociable to be left in my apartment alone. She'd just pine for Alice."

Sweet Pea complained loudly all the way to Cindy's, making it impossible to talk. When they reached the house, Dan picked up the supplies while Cindy took the cat's carrier and hurried on to the deck to open the door.

When cat and supplies were in, Dan lingered, as if he wanted to say something. He checked the roof above the door and wandered around the house to check the rest of the roof. When Cindy thought he surely must be ready to get in his van, he walked down to the lake's edge. "I can't believe it. The ice has all gone."

A skiffle of wind danced across the water's surface and ruffled Dan's fair hair. Still standing on the deck, Cindy leaned on the railing and watched him. He looked wonderful in his cream sweater and well-worn jeans. He raised his arm and tried to brush his hair back from his forehead and she squelched the urge to go to him and ask forgiveness for her lack of trust. With a sigh, she realized she just didn't have the courage. Turning back to the doorway, she said, "I'd better get Sweet Pea settled. I'll see you tomorrow at the parade."

Dan, equally at a loss as to how to resolve things, took the opportunity she threw him. "Merry's parents are coming tomorrow morning with her little boy. I thought I'd take them to supper at that restaurant over by the falls. We'll have an early meal and then head down to watch the parade. Would you come?"

Cindy, interested in meeting Merry's family and glad to have another chance, agreed.

* * *

Cindy dotted the last 'i' and crossed the last 't' on her set of winter menus. Everything was accounted for, including some specials for the Christmas season. Now, all she had to do was double-check the prices of the recipes, test new ideas she'd included and the tearoom menus would be one quarter finished.

Sweet Pea chose that moment to jump up on the table and stretch out on the menus.

"Sweet Pea," laughed Cindy. "You're incorrigible."

The small cat stretched languidly on her precious papers and purred.

"You're not getting away with being on the table." Tapping the cat gently on the nose, she said, "This is the third time this afternoon. Now scat."

Sweet Pea obviously had other ideas. The minute Cindy tried to lift her off of her project, the cat went limp. As she lifted her down, Sweet Pea did an elegant twist and landed on her lap. Then, as if to apologize for being such a pest, Sweet Pea put her paws on Cindy's shoulders and proceeded to lick her chin.

Picking a piece of scrunched-up paper off the table, Cindy waved it in front of Sweet Pea, then threw it. The cat was after it in a second. Amused, Cindy watched as Sweet Pea batted it around the hardwood floor.

When Cindy had first let the cat out of the carrier, it had cautiously examined the downstairs rooms. For a little while, it had called and Cindy was sure she was hunting for Alice. Finally she had settled down on Cindy's lap and slept.

The minute she woke, however, she was back to what Cindy thought must be her usual form. She was into everything. Every time Cindy was ready to put her back in her carrier so she could get some work done, Sweet Pea would curl up in a ball and sleep unless, of course, she wanted to torment Cindy with one of her sallies across her papers.

Looking at her watch, Cindy decided to stop for supper. Later, she would take a break from menus and seriously plan how she would furnish and decorate the sunroom and dining room of Alice's house. She intended to include hand-drawn illustrations and floor plans as well as the photographs of the house as it was now in the project.

As Cindy made a salad and warmed bread to go with chili she'd made earlier that week, she thought about Dan. But then, she thought wryly, when didn't she think about Dan. He'd lurked in her mind all the time she'd worked on her menus. If only they could break down the wall of misunderstanding. It was all very confusing.

He certainly seemed to want to be with her all time. He had even taken her to see Alice's house. Maybe she'd talk to Carolyn again. Carolyn and David had had a very rocky courtship. Maybe Carolyn could suggest a solution.

Dan sat with his guests, a smile fixed on his face. They were all enjoying themselves while he could hardly keep from grinding his teeth or possibly, if he could, spit nails. He'd done it again. And he could blame it all on that soft blue angora sweater Cindy was wearing.

It had taken considerable time for everyone to peel off the various layers of clothing they'd worn in anticipation of the parade and, even more importantly, the promised cold front. Dan had helped Merry and her mother out of their coats while Cindy had helped Merry's son Michael out of his.

In spite of his mixed feelings about Cindy, he

couldn't resist touching her when the opportunity occurred. He had been quick to assist her with her jacket. Then, he had lifted her scarf off her shoulders and his fingers had come in contact with the softness of the sweater. In spite of himself, he had been unable to resist the urge to run his fingers along the neckline, touching the sweater and then, of course overdoing it by allowing his fingers to roam to the silkiness of her nape. She had jumped like a scalded cat and hastily taken Michael's hand to lead him to a seat at the restaurant window. Good manners required Dan to let his guests have the other seats near the glass.

They had already started to eat when a voice said, "Looks like great minds think alike."

Startled, Dan turned around to see David and Carolyn settling down at the table behind them. Standing, Dan said, "Come and meet Merry and her family."

After the introductions had been made, Dan said, "Why don't we ask them to move your table next to ours?"

David groaned and Carolyn laughed, "You jest."

When everyone looked confused by the remark, David confessed, "I really can't stand heights. As it is, I'm going to sit with my back to the window just where we are. The only reason I let Carolyn drag me in here is because she adores their Chicken Parmesan."

When everyone at Dan's table had finished their first course and were waiting for dessert, Michael turned to watch the water pour over the eighty-foot curve of the falls. Almost dusk now, the setting sun slanted past the restaurant to brighten the limestone wall where the water had cut through to form the beginning of the river beyond.

Michael cried out suddenly, "Look, there's a bird sitting on the rock."

Sure enough, on the other side of the chasm was a mallard contentedly working on its feathers on a ledge about four feet above the swirling waters just beyond the eddy formed by the falls.

"It's a mallard duck," Cindy explained. "Look how he uses his beak to comb his feathers. It's a good thing he's doing it today. Tomorrow, he'd probably slide off."

The little boy's grandparents leaned over to see the bird. "What do you mean?" asked Michael's grandmother.

"Well, if we get the promised drop in temperature tonight, the moisture created by the falls will coat some of the limestone ledges. I doubt whether the ducks could perch on them."

"You mean, it might fall in?" asked Michael.

"I'm fairly sure if it slipped, it would manage to fly away," said Cindy. "I think it's far too smart to go on the ledge when it's frozen. It will want to stay in the water where it can keep its feet warm."

Michael's grandfather said, "I'm surprised to see mallards at this time of year. I would have thought they would migrate."

"Lots of birds live on the river all winter. The movement of the water keeps it from freezing over," Dan explained. "They seem to find enough to eat and of course, there are always people feeding them."

Still curious, Merry asked, "How do you suppose the mallard got there? It might be difficult to land there."

"I've seen them land. Nothing seems to faze them. However, there is another way to get there. If you look carefully, you can see that the ledge runs along and down toward the cement fishing dock on the right. In our teens, we used to wiggle up a ways on that ledge.

Not as far as the eddy but certainly about where the falls end and the river begins. If we could do it, I'm sure the mallard can do it too."

When everyone looked shocked at their teenage antics, she added hastily, "There are ledges of limestone under the water that you can't see. In the summer, it's not that deep. Although, my dad said that if he ever heard of me trying that trick, he'd ground me forever."

Then with a very mischievous grin, she added, "Fortunately, he never knew."

Dan's heart did a somersault. Immediately, the image of a grinning youngster sprang to mind; a little girl with springy curls and mischievous eyes.

Dan finished off his coffee and vowed that somehow, he had to break the stalemate they seemed to be caught in. Maybe he'd talk to David. After all, he and Carolyn had had quite a stormy courtship. Maybe David would have helpful advice.

They sat around talking until Carolyn and David had finished their meal. Then they headed out into the evening to see the parade. It began in the fairgrounds east of the village, crossed the bridge over the approach to the falls and moved along the main street. The trick was to be early enough to get a place in front of one of the stores that also supplied free treats. Dan and his group managed to get a spot in front of a stand that served hot chocolate.

Dan had brought lawn chairs for the grandparents and they were soon settled on the edge of the sidewalk with Michael on his grandfather's knee. The rest of them stood behind. Dan glanced at Cindy. She was just like a kid, stepping out every so often to check if she could see any action. The fact that she chose to stand as far away as possible didn't exactly cheer him. He wanted her beside him, tucked under his arm for warmth and support. You could go over and put your arm around her, he thought. Not without finding out where she got the crazy idea that he could drop her for Gina, he answered himself.

Finally, they heard music and one of the local brass bands appeared, led by several students with flags. Michael was entranced by the parade. Volunteers dressed as Santa's helpers came along at intervals offering all kinds of treats. One painted stars on Michael's cheeks while another had a large stocking from which the little boy pulled sweets.

As they watched, Dan asked Carolyn, "How come you weren't working out at the fairgrounds?"

"Not a chance," said Carolyn. "I want to see Santa come down the street."

It seemed every organization in town had managed to get into the parade. Sometimes it was only a convertible done up with Christmas decorations and people sitting on the edges of the seats. Other times, there were floats; some obviously homemade, others quite sophisticated. The choirs in town sat on one farmer's hay wagon and sang carols while the drug store's float boasted a large Christmas tree beautifully decorated.

Then, to everyone's surprise, a float for Dan's clinic appeared. A local farmer had offered a prize team of Clydesdale horses and his hay wagon to pull the float. The technician Mel, the student Peter, and Gina had worked on the float. Gina and Mel wore white lab coats and wrapped and unwrapped various parts of a very willing Labrador Retriever held by Peter. The crowd loved it.

Cindy turned to Dan. "When on earth did you have time to get that float ready?"

Nodding to the three people on the float, Dan said, "They did it. They had a great time." Again, Cindy realized how much Gina was a part of Dan's team in the clinic. It was difficult. To clear herself she could very easily destroy that team.

Just at that moment, a whisper of cold air snaked its way along the street. People shivered and pulled up their collars. Shivering beside Dan, Cindy said, "It feels like winter is returning."

There was a momentary pause in the procession and they all managed to get hot chocolate before it began again. Michael was getting excited about seeing Santa and wiggling up and down between and on his grandparents. To Dan's left, Carolyn was equally restless with anticipation. "Wait till you see it," she whispered to Dan. "It works just as you and David suggested."

At last the waiting was over. First the infamous float with the church and carollers came by and, much to Dan's amusement, Cindy actually glanced at her hand and gingerly fingered the spot that had been injured.

"How is it?" he asked.

"Better. I'm getting the stitches out on Monday."

A roar went up and Santa's sled came into view. It was everything Carolyn had predicted. From a distance, everyone could see Santa's sled high up in the air with the waving line of reindeer just about to settle on the float.

Michael was straining to see when Carolyn's quiet brother Andy appeared from nowhere and lifted Michael up on his shoulders. Michael was so entranced that he hardly noticed he was sitting on a stranger. Merry, on the other hand, was concerned until Carolyn said, "Don't worry. He's my brother."

Dan watched Merry relax and smile at Andy and to his amazement, Andy smiled back. Not his usual shy grin but an out-and-out smile, dimples and all. Glancing at Carolyn, he saw that she was watching with interest, then turned and grinned at David.

It was a weary but happy Michael who snuggled down on Andy's shoulder. As the group of them headed for the SUV, he murmured, "I'm going to be a good boy, Mummy, so Santa can find me Christmas Eve."

When they reached the restaurant parking lot, Andy lifted an exhausted Michael into the safety seat. Again, Andy favored Merry with one of his smiles and said, "You have a great little guy."

As they drove back to the bed and breakfast, Merry's mother asked Dan, "Who was that stranger that held on to Michael?"

"He's Carolyn's brother." Then as an afterthought, he added, "I've never seen Andy smile like that. He's very shy."

"He has a ponytail," observed Merry's mother.

"Of course he has," said Merry. "He looks just like Carolyn. The same blue eyes and dark hair." After a pause, she added, "They are a handsome family."

Dan couldn't resist looking at Cindy and raising his eyebrows at this remark. She grinned back.

After taking Merry and her family home, Dan headed out to Cindy's place. Away from the village lights, the night was beautiful. A full moon jeweled the branches of the leafless trees and lit a path across the lake. When they got out of the SUV, they both stood spellbound, hardly daring to breathe for fear the whiteness of their breath would somehow shatter the splendor.

What a night for taking the woman you love in your arms, Dan thought sadly. They needed to talk but he was exhausted. Until they did, he intended to ignore such a romantic setting. Anyway, the way she'd jumped when he'd removed her scarf suggested that she would not welcome such an advance.

Saying good night and hopping in the van, Dan headed back to the clinic to see if Mel and Gina needed any help straightening up.

Disappointed, Cindy walked through the moonlight up onto the deck and let herself into the house. Even Sweet Pea's delight at her return did little to get her attention. She'd wanted to confront him but the moonlight had taken the wind our of her sails. In the mystery of its glow, she'd been ready to forget explanations and to kiss and make up. Obviously he hadn't.

Tonight, he had touched her like a lover. The moment was so unexpected that she'd been startled. Somehow, she'd expected him to follow up his advance here in the moonlight.

Looking outside, she thought, it is every woman's dream to be kissed on a night like this. Last summer, Dan had taken every opportunity to do that very thing on every moonlit night that had presented itself. Shaking her head, she picked up Sweet Pea and went to the kitchen to feed her. When the cat had finished, she headed upstairs, the calico dancing before her. "The sooner I see Carolyn, the better," she told Sweet Pea.

When Dan reached the clinic, Mel and Gina were just loading the two horses into the horse trailer for the farmer. Often on display, the horses were used to the trailer and trotted into their stalls without any trouble.

Dan got out of his SUV and walked over to their owner, Hal Martin. Shaking his hand, he said, "Your Clydesdales were a hit as usual. I can't thank you enough. I owe you one, Hal."

"Forget it, Dan. Remember, it was a chance for me to show off my horses. I'll come back for the hay wagon tomorrow."

With that, he hopped in his truck and headed off.

Dan hurried into the clinic to help Mel and Gina finish tidying up. Mel's golden Lab Sunny was following him around as Mel wound up the bandages they'd used. Gina was hanging up the lab coats they'd worn. "You two did a good job tonight. The float was a hit. Do you have time for a cup of coffee or hot chocolate before you go home?"

Mel shook his head. "It's my day off tomorrow. I'm going to Toronto to see a Maple Leaf game. I want to get an early start. Thanks anyway."

Dan looked at Gina. "Would you like a cup of coffee?"

"Sure, Dan. I'll come in your office when I'm finished here."

Dan headed to his office to put on the coffee pot. He was glad Gina had decided to stay. He needed to talk to her. He'd been so involved with Cindy that he'd forgotten all about Gina over the past few days. He realized that there was no excuse for his behavior.

When Gina came in, he had the coffee ready along with cream and sugar that he knew she used. He also had some cookies on a plate. What would I do without coffee and cookies, he mused.

Handing her a mug of coffee and waiting until she'd settled on the chair across from the desk, he said, "Thanks for being such a help tonight, Gina."

Gina shrugged. "It was nothing. We had fun."

They both sipped their coffee. Gina took a cookie and nibbled at it while Dan tried to choose his words carefully. Finally, he began. "Gina, you know that we have spent quite a lot of time together this fall."

He watched the color drain from her face. She nodded nervously. It was going to be worse than he thought. "You must also have figured out that something is going on between Cindy Howard and myself."

Again, Gina nodded.

"I hope I never led you on, Gina. I certainly never made you any promises. I have enjoyed your friendship."

"But that's all it is?" asked Gina in a tight little voice.

"I'm afraid so. It has always been Cindy. I fell in love with her the first time I saw her. I'm still not sure why she disappeared out of my life last August. She hasn't told me yet. But I intend to find out. I hope to marry her if she'll have me."

Gina stood up. Her voice had the slightest tremor as she said, "You're right. You never made any promises. I hope you will be very happy, Dan." She turned and left the office.

Dan slumped back in his chair. He felt like a real heel.

Outside, Gina got in her car and started it. Easing it out of the clinic parking lot, she drove down the road until she was out of sight of the clinic and then parked the car and turned it off. She didn't cry although she wanted to. Putting her arms on the steering wheel, she leaned her forehead on them. She was in such a mess. Dan was right, he'd never made any promises. She'd done all the pursuing, hoping that in time he'd forget Cindy.

Jealousy had made her do the only dishonest thing she'd ever done in her life. She'd told Cindy all those terrible lies. When Dan found out what she'd done, she'd lose her job. At that, she did burst into tears. She loved her job. She liked meeting the clients, loved the animals and enjoyed being in charge. It was the best job she'd ever had. Dan had treated her with respect and appreciation. What ever could she do to make it right?

Chapter Six

All day Sunday, Monday and Tuesday, the weather remained cold and strong winds made it seem even colder. While the lake was covered with white caps and the wind rattled the house windows, Cindy worked steadily at her project, only taking breaks to bake. Tuesday night, the wind dropped suddenly and the sky cleared. When she went to bed, the lake was a still dark presence reflecting the lights of homes on the other side. During the three days, she had no contact with Dan nor had she gone in to see Crash.

Wednesday morning, Cindy opened the bedroom curtains to a brilliant blue sky and a frozen lake. Dressing quickly, she hurried to check the outside thermometer. It was two degrees above zero. Curious to know how thick the ice was, she slipped into her jacket, hat and boots and made her way to the lake's edge. The ice was as clear as glass. Through it, she could see the sand, sculpted into waves, with pebbles glinting like jewels in the sunlight. Cautiously, she tapped her toe on the surface. It was solid. Amazing, she thought as she walked across its hard surface, gazing at the unexpected world beneath.

After breakfast, Cindy settled down to check her plans for Dan's open house. There had already been an advertisement in the local weekly newspaper, *The Stewart's Falls Gazette,* inviting people in the village and surrounding areas to visit the clinic and meet Merry.

As suggested, Cindy would make lots of sandwiches. She had already made all of the squares and some of the cookies during the last three days when she needed a break from her project. However, she wanted to add something special to the trays that were passed. She'd certainly make the little Thai spring rolls. She could also make wonton with spicy meat centers.

Cindy had already contacted the students Carolyn recommended and they had agreed to serve and also to come in Friday after school to make sandwiches and discuss routines. When she finished her list of food and other items she needed, she decided to have lunch and then go to town.

Just then, the phone rang. It was Dan. Her heart turned a cartwheel when she heard his voice. "I wondered if you were free for a little while this afternoon?"

She thought about it for a moment. She'd finished with the organization of her work. It would depend on just how long he wanted. Glad to hear his voice, she said cautiously, "What do you have in mind?"

"I have a favor to ask of you," he continued. "Merry is heavily booked this afternoon and I've just been called out on an emergency. I was going to exercise

Crash for a while but haven't got time. Could you come in and spend a half hour with him? He's able to get out of the cage now and play a bit as long as he takes it easy."

Now that was something she'd really enjoy. "Sure, I'd love to but I'll need to be through by two o'clock."

"That's great." There was a pause. "How's the work going? I haven't phoned you because I knew you had a lot to do."

"I've very nearly finished all the food planning in the project."

As Cindy hung up the phone, she thought, Well, at least he knows I'm alive and is interested in my work. That should mean something.

Making a hasty lunch, Cindy was just able to reach the clinic by one o'clock. Crash was delighted to see her. Cindy had brought some puppy treats with the hope that she might be able to train him.

Opening the door, Cindy carefully lifted Crash down and steadied him while he got his balance on his three legs and splint. She needn't have worried about his balance. He was quite able to manage on three feet. There was more danger he would fall over because his tail was wagging so much when he tried to climb into her lap and lick her face all at the same time.

Laughing, she stood and watched him gambol up and down the hall. Taking some of the treats, she began to try to teach him to 'sit'. It was fun. It didn't matter that Crash got far more treats than he deserved.

Just about the time she was ready to put him back in the cage, he suddenly flopped down beside her and went to sleep. Oh, to be able to go to sleep like that, she thought. The night before, she'd been awake for hours, trying to figure out how to settle things with Dan.

Cindy put the puppy back in his cage and left him sleeping. Saying hello to Merry as she rushed from one examining room to another, Cindy put on her jacket, hat and boots, and slipped outside into the cold. Glancing at her watch, she saw that it was only two. She still had lots of time to go to the village grocer and get some supplies.

When she'd completed her shopping, she headed for the checkout counter. A voice behind her said, "I've been trying to get you on the phone."

Recognizing Carolyn's voice, Cindy turned and smiled. "What was on your mind?"

"I wondered if you'd noticed the lake."

"You mean the fact that it's frozen?"

"Not just that," said Carolyn. "When did you leave home?"

"Just before one," Cindy replied.

"Well," said Carolyn, "I think the feathers appeared after that."

"Feathers?" asked Cindy, wondering if Carolyn was setting up some kind of joke.

"Snow feathers." When Cindy didn't respond, Carolyn said, "Haven't you ever seen snow feathers?"

Cindy shook her head.

"Well, I'm not going to tell you what they are. Just hurry home and check the lake. If you don't know what I mean by then, give me a ding. It may be that you're too late to see them."

Carolyn refused to budge when Cindy coaxed for more information. In the end, she took Carolyn's advice and hurried home. Not even stopping to take her shopping into the house, she walked toward the lake. To her amazement, she saw that the ice was white.

She wasn't sure how it could be. It hadn't snowed and the sky was a vivid blue.

When she got closer, she realized that the lake wasn't actually covered with snow. Instead, there were thousands of tiny ice feathers standing up, side by side, on the surface of the lake. Kneeling down, she touched one of the fragile feathers and it crumbled. Checking the others, she saw that they were made of tiny snow crystals. They stood about the height of a double-A battery.

Starting to get cold, Cindy returned to her car to get her supplies. Just as she entered the house, the telephone rang. Dumping the parcels, she hurried to answer it.

"I finished out at the Watsons'," Dan said, "and was heading home when I noticed a strange phenomenon on their creek. The water was frozen solid when I first went out, then it was covered in what I thought was snow. But the sky was blue and there hadn't been any snow."

Cindy smiled to herself and just listened.

"I got out of the SUV and took a look. The creek was covered with tiny little ice feathers. I've never seen anything like it. I wondered if your lake had any?"

"I saw them. I ran into Carolyn in town, and she told me to go home and check for them. The lake is covered with them. They're really quite beautiful. I wonder what caused them to form?"

"I think there was a very gentle breeze today that drove cold air over the ice. Because it's so new, it's not as solid as it looks. I think the breeze picked up the moisture from tiny bubbles of air in the ice and froze it into crystals."

"I wonder how long they'll last?"

"I suppose until a strong wind comes up. By the way, how did you enjoy your time with Crash?"

"We really had fun, Dan. I'm amazed how well he manages on that splint. I was careful to see that he didn't reinjure his side." Cindy paused, and then added, "Er, I'm afraid I may have given him quite a few puppy treats. I was trying to train him to sit. I thought that might keep him from running around."

"I doubt you could give him enough treats in that short time to make him sick. By the way, did you get him to do it?"

"Once or twice."

"Well, I'd better let you get back to whatever you were doing. Just wanted to be sure you didn't miss the feathers." A prolonged pause. Then he asked, "What did you work at today?"

"I planned the food for the open house."

"Don't forget what I said," Dan cautioned. "Just make ordinary sandwiches and cookies. Don't fuss."

"Dan," Cindy said firmly. "Let me do my job the way I know best. Don't worry. I won't serve them chocolate-covered apricots or candied grasshoppers."

"That's not what I was worried about and you know it. Just because this is a trade-off between my caring for Crash and you doing the catering, I don't want you spending money and time on things that are unnecessary."

Cindy rolled her eyes. "Dan," she assured him. "I am not going overboard. In fact, I've hired two high-school students as servers and they're also going to help me make the sandwiches to save me time."

"Good," he said. "See you," and hung up.

Cindy made her favorite pizza for supper. As she ate, she dangled a piece of pizza with a small bit of anchovy over Sweet Pea's nose. "This will either cure you of begging, Sweet Pea, or make you the weirdest cat in the world. Alice must have shared every meal with you."

Sweet Pea stood on her back legs and adroitly caught the piece of pizza with her paw. Carefully, she nibbled the cheese and anchovy and then the rest. Cindy shook her head in amazement. She had yet to find anything the cat disliked.

Dan wandered around his kitchen, peeked in the fridge and then in the freezer. Nothing caught his interest. Fish and chips. That's what he'd have tonight. Fish and chips. Getting his jacket, he headed out.

He wasn't inside the small restaurant on the main street a minute when he heard his name called. Turning, he saw Carolyn and David gesturing that he should join them. He couldn't do it fast enough. Maybe he'd get a chance to speak to David alone.

Of course, both Reids were interested when they saw that Dan was without Cindy. How come? They glanced at each other, trying to send ideas back and forth.

As Dan settled, Carolyn asked, "Did you see the snow feathers?"

"Yes."

That didn't tell her much. "Where did you see them?"

"Out at Watsons' farm."

Now why did Carolyn look disappointed, he wondered.

She continued. "I thought you might have seen them out at Cindy's place. I ran into her at the grocers and told her about them."

David nudged her under the table and she jumped slightly.

"I phoned Cindy about the snow feathers," Dan said, "but she'd already seen them."

At that point the waitress brought the Reids' order. Turning to Dan, she said, "Want the same?"

"I certainly would," he replied.

Before the waitress could move away, Carolyn asked, "How's your little boy these days, Ruth?"

"He's not doing badly but he is getting too much for my mother. It would be so much better if I could stay home with him but it's just not possible."

When Ruth left, Carolyn said, "I just wish there was something we could do for Ruth. She's such a fine person. She's too young to be left a widow. It's too bad she couldn't find a job where she could work at home and be with her son."

While they waited for their food, Dan entertained them with an incident he'd had that day trying to catch a parakeet that got loose in the clinic. After that they discussed the parade and especially the Santa float.

Then, quite out of the blue, David said, "I've been thinking that we might have an impromptu skating party tomorrow night."

Dan was amused by Carolyn's face. First she had looked surprised and then had quickly tried to hide her reaction. She's a good sport, thought Dan, ready to support David even if the idea was completely new to her.

Carolyn, after her initial surprise, lit up with enthusiasm. "What a good idea. You'd be able to come, wouldn't you, Dan?"

"Short of emergencies, yes. But where do you intend to skate?"

"On our lake," said David. "The ice is already thick enough to support everyone's weight. It will be even thicker tomorrow. The ice feathers will have disappeared by then. A good breeze or the morning sun will finish them."

Remembering that the Reids' house was up on a hill above the lake, Dan asked, "How will you get people down to the lake!"

"I've got that all figured out," said David. "I'll use my plow."

"He just loves that plow," Carolyn teased. Then she added, "We have power down there. We'll get Andy to string up some lights. We can have a fire and roast marshmallows. We'll have a wonderful time. As soon as we've finished here, I'll go home and start phoning people."

Dan was amused listening to them as between each mouthful, they thought of another thing to do. He couldn't help observing, "It's a good thing you two are on holiday for the entire month. You'd never pull this off if you were working."

Both Carolyn and David said, "Wanna bet?"

When it was time to go, Dan said, "Thanks for letting me join you. It was just what I needed. I was feeling a little lonely tonight."

Before they could ask inquisitive but sympathetic Cupid questions, Dan said, "I've just had an idea. Merry needs a housekeeper and someone to care for her little boy. How about Ruth? Isn't her son about the same age?"

"That's a wonderful idea," said Carolyn.

"Well, let me talk to Merry first. Maybe she could come in here sometime and meet Ruth." Turning to David, Dan said, "Could you drop into the clinic tomorrow sometime?" Noticing Carolyn's interest, he grinned at her and said, "Man talk." Which was true enough, but he also wanted David to look at Crash.

As Dan headed out of the restaurant, Carolyn whispered to her husband, "We have to make sure Cindy comes to the party. Even if I have to go over and help her with whatever she's making for the open house."

He laughed. Although Carolyn was an excellent cook and had run her father's home for years, he knew she'd much rather make models and leave the cooking to him. Something he'd only recently become interested in. "Now, that is a real sacrifice for the cause."

Dan had just finished the morning surgery when David arrived. "Come to see Crash?" Dan asked.

"That and whatever man-to-man talk you want although I have to warn you, my wife is dying of curiosity."

Dan looked appalled. "You won't tell her?"

David thought for a moment, then grinned. "I promise. Although it won't be easy. Where's Crash?"

"Right through here." Dan led the way to the large cage where the puppy sat chewing at a piece of hide.

Opening the door, Dan reached in and lifted the puppy out and gently placed him on the floor. Crash immediately got up on his three legs and splint and headed for David's foot. As they watched, he tackled the laces on David's hikers.

Squatting down to see the puppy better, David asked, "How's his leg and side healing?"

"His side is nearly back to normal and his leg is knitting just fine. Although I'll have to change the splint again soon. He's growing like a bad weed."

Delighted with this new stranger who seemed interested in him, Crash stood on his hind legs and tried to lick David's face.

"He's a charming little guy," said David. "Do you think he'll be well enough to leave here by Christmas?"

Relieved, Dan said, "I don't see why not. I could bring him out Christmas Day if you like."

David nodded, "I'd like that very much. I can buy lots of things for the puppy as extra gifts for Carolyn. She can open them when you all are there in the afternoon."

Picking up the puppy, David stood up. "He's a sturdy little guy. You've looked after him well, Dan. He's a lot luckier than the pup that's haunting the stores on the main street. I gather people are leaving food out for it on the chance they can get close enough to catch it. It's a little female. The druggist seems to be having some success. The puppy has a good meal each morning when he opens and again when he closes. Unfortunately, she still won't let Phil get close enough to catch her."

Dan frowned. "You know, she managed during the past warm spell but I don't see how she can possibly survive if it gets much colder." Taking some treats from his lab coat pocket, he said, "Put Crash down and see if he'll sit. Cindy said she tried to teach him how yesterday."

David placed Crash on the floor and took the treats from Dan. Patiently he said "Sit" and held the tidbit up for the puppy to smell. All Crash would do was follow David's hand with his nose.

Kneeling, Dan called Crash who came gamboling over. Holding the puppy still and pushing down his bottom, he said, "Sit." When the puppy stayed for a few seconds, he said, "Good boy," and gave him a treat. He tried it again and the puppy allowed himself to be positioned and held the stance. Again, Dan said, "Good boy," and gave him the treat.

Looking at David, he said, "He's bright. This is a new game to him. Try it."

Dan watched as David put the puppy through his paces. By then, Dan could see that Crash had won David's heart. "You could come in here whenever someone is around and try to teach him some other things. We're already starting to train him to do his business outside. Think how impressed Carolyn will be when she gets a well-trained puppy. I'll lend you a book."

Looking up, David asked, "Would you mind?"

"Not at all. Anyway, that would save Cindy from coming over to exercise him. I think she's pretty busy getting ready for the open house."

David picked up the puppy and put him back in his cage. "How are things going between you two?"

"Come and have coffee," Dan said. "I have a patient in twenty minutes but I could use a break."

David followed Dan into his office, all his Cupid instincts alert.

Dan sighed and said, "You asked how things were going between Cindy and me."

"Well," David said, "I know it's none of my business. But it hurts to see two friends so at odds."

Dan looked surprised. "Is it that obvious?"

"Yes."

David took a sip of the coffee Dan handed him and watched his friend pour one for himself. He still found it hard to understand how a terrific guy like Dan hadn't won Carolyn's heart but Carolyn had said that they'd only been good friends. Curiosity drove him to say, "Carolyn said there was never any spark between you two."

Dan couldn't resist a smile. "You asked, did you?"

"Well, I have to admit that I had the occasional lack of confidence at first where you were concerned. I couldn't quite believe that Carolyn would prefer me to your Hollywood good looks."

Dan snorted at that and then sobered. "Carolyn and I were just friends. It was convenient for us to squire each other to social occasions and, of course, I enjoyed playing tennis with her."

He paused and had he but known it, he got a soppy look on his face. "I took one look at Cindy that night in the coffee shop and that was it. And I thought it was the same for her."

"What happened?"

"She just disappeared after she got home from Nova Scotia last August. She didn't even come and see me before she left. I knew she'd returned and expected to see her after work that day but when I went out to her parents' place, she was gone. Her mother told me she'd left for school. I think her mother thought I'd done something wrong."

"Have you asked Cindy why she left?"

Dan's eyes glinted. "I certainly did."

"And?"

"I discovered she didn't trust me. How would you have felt if Carolyn hadn't trusted you when you were falling love?"

"I don't know. Carolyn and I had much different problems. I couldn't stand women who wore work-boots and did men's jobs. She had no use for academics. Seems her fingers were burnt once by such a type. Anyway," David said with a grin, "you know all about our stormy courtship. It seems to me you thought the entire thing was hilarious."

"Well. You don't see me laughing now, do you."

David finished his coffee and stood up. "Look, it's obvious you love Cindy. I'm also sure you know what you have to do. I'm sure nothing I can tell you will alter that fact. I'll see you tonight, I hope. Maybe on a moonlit night you might just find the courage to do it."

Dan watched him disappear through the door. David was right. He did know what he had to do. He had to come off his high horse and admit to Cindy that he'd overreacted. Maybe he could do it tonight.

Cindy was just taking the last pan of chocolate chip cookies out of the oven when she heard a rap on the door. Putting the tray down, she checked out the window to see who had arrived. Immediately she recognized the Reids' truck. Curious, she opened the door for Carolyn.

Hurrying in, Carolyn shivered as she pulled off her hat and unwrapped the scarf she had wound around her neck. "That is cold," she announced. "We're going to freeze to death tonight unless that wind stops. Fortunately, the weather channel said it will drop off later today."

Taking Carolyn's coat and hanging it up, Cindy said, "What do you have on tonight that's going to have you going outside?"

Instead of answering her, Carolyn headed for the kitchen. "H-mmm. What is that glorious smell?"

"Cookies. You can have some. I'll just make some fresh coffee."

Amused by Carolyn's mysterious visit, Cindy made coffee and waited for Carolyn's answer to her initial question.

Carolyn asked, "How's the baking coming?"

Okay, thought Cindy. I'll play your game. "That's the last of the cookies. I've made three kinds, all guaranteed not to crumble on the clinic floor."

Cindy piled cookies of all three types on a plate and

handed them to Carolyn. "Help yourself. The coffee will be ready in a minute."

"What else have you got to do for Saturday?"

"Not a lot," said Cindy. "The students you recommended are coming over Friday right after school to make sandwiches so I have the fillings to make."

Carolyn took another cookie.

Finally running out of patience, Cindy said, "Okay Carolyn, what's up that you're so interested in my schedule?"

Looking very guilty, Carolyn said, "I admit I have an ulterior motive. I'm having a skating party tonight on the lake below our house. It's frozen as smooth as glass just like yours is. That doesn't happen very often so I thought it was a good time to enjoy it. Everyone is coming and I hope you will, too."

When Cindy poured herself some coffee instead of giving her answer right away, Carolyn added, "Andy's connecting fairy lights down there and we're going to have hot chocolate and marshmallows. That's why I asked so many questions. I was going to offer to help you if you were swamped with work. Say you'll come."

Cindy glanced at Carolyn. Just what was she up to, she wondered? On the other hand, Cindy loved skating.

"Of course, I'll come. I'm ready for a break from cooking. And you can relax. I really don't need help but I appreciate the offer."

Relieved, Carolyn picked up a chocolate chip cookie, bit into it and crooned with delight. "That is a cookie to die for. What did you do to it?"

Very pleased with her reaction, Cindy explained, "It's an experiment. I plan to use the recipe in my tearoom project. Out of curiosity, would you come to a tearoom for afternoon cookies if I served those?"

"Every day," exclaimed Carolyn and grabbed another.

At that point, Sweet Pea, who must have been sleeping upstairs, came bouncing into the room. "Who have we here?" asked Carolyn.

"Sweet Pea," answered Cindy. "She's Alice Thornton's cat. I said I'd take care of her until Dan finds a home for her."

Sweet Pea chose that moment to chase a piece of nut that had fallen to the floor. She leaped straight up in the air and turned arabesques with gay abandon. "I wonder," said Carolyn, "whether Merry would like her for her little boy. She told me that she worries about him. He still seems a trifle lost with all the upsets in his life."

"That's a good idea," said Cindy. "Suggest it to Dan."

"Mm-m, how are things going between you two?"

Carolyn was not encouraged when Cindy frowned, got up and walked over to the coffee pot again. "Not so well. Dan accused me of not trusting him."

"Why was that?"

"Well, he asked me why I went away. Instead of telling him about the things Gina had said, I asked him whether he'd had a good time with Gina in Ottawa. He hit the roof."

"So why don't you tell him what Gina said?"

Cindy sighed. "At first, I was just broken-hearted. I realized I had spoiled things between us. He was absolutely right. I should never have believed Gina without checking the facts." Cindy could feel the tears threatening, her throat tightening. She swallowed. "Then I got mad. He didn't ask me why I was so sure of my facts. After I cooled down about that, I realized that that was just an excuse. I knew Dan. I should never have believed Gina and run away."

"Well, you know what you have to do, don't you?"

Blinking back tears, Cindy said, "You mean tell Dan and confront Gina?"

Carolyn nodded.

"It's not so simple now. I've seen how much Dan depends on Gina at the clinic. She really makes it a pleasant place to bring your pet. She's kind to the clients and loves the animals. She certainly keeps Dan's day organized. I swear she loves her job and I'm sure she thinks she loves Dan."

"But she lied," reminded Carolyn.

"Yes, she broke his trust and I know just how he'll react to that fact. I'll tell Dan. I just have to figure out a way."

Standing up and taking her coffee mug to the sink, Carolyn said, "I'm sure you'll do it. Maybe you should talk to Gina first. Get her to admit what she did to Dan. Anyway, come tonight, Cindy. I imagine Dan is coming if he can manage it. Oh, by the way, would you have an extra pair of skates, size seven? I invited Merry but her skates are back in Toronto."

"I'm pretty sure I can find a pair. I'll let Merry know at the clinic if I can locate them."

Carolyn got up and headed for the door. As she picked up her coat, she paused. "What would you think of Ruth Winston as a babysitter for Merry's little boy? It would mean that she could be with her own little guy at the same time. Maybe she could do some light housekeeping, too."

Cindy thought for a moment. "I think that might be a very good idea. I'm sure my parents wouldn't mind.

They did suggest that Merry would have room for a live-in housekeeper."

"Well, it was Dan's idea. He's going to suggest Merry go in and meet Ruth at the restaurant." Bundling up, Carolyn headed out into the cold. "See you tonight."

Dan's last appointment was with a very nasty little hamster who took great joy in biting anything he could get his teeth into. Closing the door of the examining room behind its owner, a ten-year-old girl, he leaned against it and shut his eyes. What a day. Gina was out in the reception room, white-faced and subdued. The entire clinic seemed affected by her gloom. She'd just announced when she'd brought in the little girl with her hamster that she needed to see him when they closed. She was probably going to quit.

He rubbed the back of his neck as he headed to his office. Stopping at the door to the reception, he called through, "Anytime you're ready, Gina, I'm in my office."

Gina came in almost immediately. "Have a seat," Dan said, and walked around to his own chair behind his desk. "What can I do for you?"

To his dismay, Gina burst into tears. Grabbing some tissues, he headed around the desk again and thrust them toward her. She grabbed one and then sobbed, "You're going to hate me."

Still feeling like the biggest heel in the world, Dan said gently, "I told you last night, you were my friend. How could I hate you?"

She rocked back and forth, her arms tight around her middle. "You don't know. I've done something unforgivable. You'll never want to see me again."

Truly worried now, all kinds of weird scenarios

flashed through Dan's mind; she'd stolen drugs? taken money? Dismissing such ideas as nonsense, he pulled up a chair beside her and said gently, "Tell me what's wrong, Gina."

Looking at him through her tears, she said, "I'm the reason Cindy left you."

That focused his attention. "Explain, Gina."

"I'm so sorry. I love my job and I know you're going to fire me."

"Explain why you are the reason Cindy left me."

Gina sat back and between hiccups, said, "I thought I was in love with you and I thought you were beginning to care for me. When I heard she'd returned, I went to see her at work. I told her all kinds of lies."

Gina took a second to blow her nose, and then between shuddering sobs, she continued. "I told her you'd taken me to your cousin's wedding. You'd told me about it on the way home from Ottawa and I saw the pictures. I could describe the colors of the dresses the bridesmaids wore and all the details of the bride's gown. I also said we'd gone to Ottawa for a holiday together. Cindy couldn't help but believe me."

Dan was speechless. He wanted to wring his sorry receptionist's little neck.

"I wanted to make her jealous." Looking at him through her tears, she said, "I'm so sorry Dan. I didn't stop to think things through. I never meant to make you so unhappy. I never wanted to lose my job here. I realize now that I was just infatuated."

Well, thank God for that, he thought. At least one good thing had come out of this confession. He hadn't broken her heart. But she'd nearly broken his. He thought for a few minutes while Gina snuffled away in her tissues, still hiccuping occasionally.

"Would you apologize to Cindy?"

Gina nodded.

Finally, Dan decided what to do. "Look at me, Gina."

She blew her nose and straightened to watch him anxiously.

"I am sorry I didn't realize how you felt last summer. I would never have encouraged you." He paused for a moment to find the right words. "What you did nearly destroyed two lives. You do understand that?"

She nodded.

"Gina," he went on. "You are the best receptionist I have ever had. You make the clinic a pleasant place to be. You are kind and patient with the clients and love their pets. I value that and don't want to lose you. Let's make a deal. First, you apologize to Cindy. Second, we have a month trial period at work. If we are both convinced that we can work after this, then as far as I am concerned, the job is still yours. Fair enough?"

He could see the relief flood her face as she nodded. "Okay, Gina, I'll see you tomorrow. Will you lock up the front? I have to have supper in a hurry so I'll see you tomorrow." With that, he left her to herself.

David placed a big urn of hot chocolate on the back of the truck's tailgate and plugged into the extension Andy had rigged up. Looking around, he decided his idea was a success. To begin with, it was a perfect evening for a skating party. Moonlight shimmered across the expanse of frozen lake, creating a wonderland of silver that touched the trees on the shore and lit the faces of the skaters. Nature, he thought, seemed to be encouraging his ventures.

Everyone they'd asked had come except Gina. She had said she wasn't sure she could make it. Almost all of Carolyn's family were there and most of those who were in the tennis club and those who had put on the play in the summer were present. A very enthusiastic Henry was skating with Margaret whenever he could. And miracle of miracles, Andy was there, helping Carolyn and, he was sure, waiting for just the right moment to ask Merry to skate. Most important was the fact that Cindy and Dan had come, separately but at least they were there.

David sensed a determination in Dan this evening. He had politely partnered Merry and Margaret and a few of the other tennis players. Now he headed toward Cindy who was gliding along beside Henry.

David poured himself a Styrofoam cup of hot chocolate and looked around for Carolyn. Just then, Ben, Carolyn's youngest brother, arrived and proudly presented David with a ghetto blaster and some CD's. "Help me connect this so we can have music." A minute later, his wife was there with a small ladder she'd insisted they bring down. Shaking his head at the instinctive way she could hone in on an opportunity to climb, he said, "I'll hold you while you stand on this device. It's too slippery to take a chance."

Reaching up and giving him a peck on the cheek, she said, "Thank you, darling. I'd appreciate that." Diverted by his wife's unexpected agreement, David forgot to watch Dan.

Dan made his way to shore and poured himself a cup of hot chocolate. He watched Cindy and Henry skating along the shore, deep in conversation. He was going to take David's advice. He'd even found a romantic spot just down the lake where he could admit he'd overreacted.

Dan shook his head with amazement. Seven months ago, he wouldn't have believed that he would be mooning after a woman he loved. Even five months ago, he wouldn't have believed that anything could have spoiled the wonderful thing that had happened between Cindy and himself. He watched Cindy and Henry part and Cindy head for the hot chocolate urn. Quickly he poured her a cup and headed out to meet her.

When he reached her, he said, "Like a cup?"

She did a half turn on her skates and held out her hand. "Sure. Great party, isn't it?"

They started to skate slowly along the shore in the direction of the quiet cove Dan had selected.

"It is now," Dan said.

She looked at him and frowned. "What do you mean?"

By now, they were out of sight of the others. "I mean that now that I'm skating with you, the party is great."

Cindy skated on in silence. She didn't seem impressed. How was he going to have his say when she was determined to ignore his compliment? He tried again, "Slow down, Cindy. I have something important to say."

"About Crash?"

He tried to muffle a sigh. "No, not about Crash. About us."

That got her attention. "Us?"

He reached over and tried to take her hand at the same time she reversed so that she was facing him.

In a funny voice, she said, "Is there an 'us'?"

Dan could feel panic rising. He had to do this right. The darn moonlight was too bright and Cindy was obviously choosing to be obtuse. She was skating backward too quickly. If she didn't take care, she'd trip and break her neck.

"For heaven sake," Dan snapped. "Would you please stop skating."

She did a quick turn and slid to stop, sending a spray of ice toward him. Folding her arms over her chest, she said, "Well?"

"Well what?" He was losing the thread of the conversation.

"I asked you what you meant by 'us'."

Her face was porcelain white in the moonlight, her curls silvered. Her eyes glittered with emotion. He ached to take her in his arms, kiss the nervous look in her eyes away and tell her he loved her.

He was about to reached for her when he heard Gina call, "Cindy, Dan. Wait up."

If it was possible for an adult to have a tantrum, Dan would have had it then. He wanted to stretch out on the ice and kick his heels in sheer frustration. Taking a big breath to steady himself, he turned toward Gina. "Yes, Gina. What is it?"

Gina skated slowly up to them. Cindy folded her arms across her chest and waited.

"Cindy," Gina said, looking her straight in the eye. "I want to apologize for lying to you. I never went to Dan's cousin's wedding. We never went on a holiday in Ottawa. I made it all up. I was jealous." Her voice trembled as she continued. "I know you love Dan and that he loves you. I'm sorry."

With that, she fled.

They both stood like statues, watching her disappear around the point toward the sound of music and laughter.

Turning toward Cindy, Dan said, "She confessed after work tonight." Reaching over, he took her hands and pulled her nearer. "Why didn't you tell me what she'd said?"

Cindy blurted out, "I was hurt. Then, when I'd re-alized how badly I'd treated you when I didn't trust you, I was ashamed. I didn't know how to tell you. I knew Gina was important to the clinic. I thought you might fire her."

Dan hauled her into his arms and held her tightly. Into her taffy curls, he confessed, "And I overreacted. I shouldn't have gone all self-righteous. I should have explained that I just drove Gina to her sister's. I at-tended a symposium and met a fellow veterinarian from New Zealand. I had nothing else to do while you were away. I missed you."

In the moonlight now, her face glowed and her eyes had a light in them he hadn't seen in months. Taking her face in his hands, he traced her eyes, her nose and then her lips with his fingers. "I love you," he mur-mured. She reached up and pulled his head down until their lips met and they were lost in sheer delight. He heard voices coming nearer and he pulled them into the shadow of a huge willow and deepened the kiss. She responded, clinging to him as if she would never let him go again.

But the voices came closer yet, and it slowly dawned on each of them that their friends had formed a tango line. Within seconds they were discovered and the line circled them, cheering and insisting they join. Taking Cindy by the waist, Dan turned her and pushed her to the end of the line. With a laugh of resignation, she reached out and grabbed Margaret's waist. "We'll finish this later," Dan yelled.

It was with dismay that Carolyn and David followed in the line that had intruded on the lovers. None of their other friends had realized the significance of find-ing them in each other's arms. Over the next half hour, the group seemed inspired to think up things to do that involved everyone. It wasn't until Caroline had the inspiration to find a tape of waltzes, that the two lovers managed to get together again.

Laughing, Dan caught Cindy's hand as the Skaters' Waltz began. "Maybe we can get lucky and dance our way back down the lake. I liked that place beneath the willow."

With a beatific smile on her face, Cindy nodded. She was sure her skates hardly touched the ice as they glided along. When they reached the protection of the tree, she turned to Dan, When he went to reach for her, she held up her hand. "Let me say this first, Dan Hamilton. I love you."

That's all he'd ever wanted to hear. They fell into each other's arms, kissing each other until Dan finally grumbled, "Why couldn't we have solved our problems in a warm place. C'mon. I'm taking you home."

They skated back, changed into their hikers and started up the hill. Slowly, many of the other skaters followed. After all, the next day was a work day. Andy unhooked the power and then, instead of helping Carolyn and David pack up, surprised them by heading out on the ice again.

He made his way down the ice in the opposite direction to the way Dan and Cindy had gone, checking along the shore. Finally, he found what he was looking for. Huddled on a rock protruding out of the ice was Gina. Andy skated up to her and held out his hand. "It's time to go," he said. When she didn't move, he leaned forward and with his finger, lifted her chin. "Gina?"

He wasn't surprised when he saw tears on her face and ice on her mittens where she'd brushed them away. She closed her eyes and tried to turn her face away. Gently, he said, "You can't make people love you, Gina. It just has to happen naturally."

With a shudder, Gina whispered, "I know that now. That's not why I'm hiding away out here."

Andy didn't say anything. He just waited. Finally, Gina said in a desperate voice, "I'm a terrible person. I did an awful thing. I told lies. I've never done it before." With a shake of her head, she said, "I'll never do it again."

Taking her hand and pulling her to her feet, Andy said, "Love can make us all do things we regret, Gina. You have to learn to forgive yourself. Come now, skate with me back to the truck. Carolyn and David are getting ready to leave."

Then, without a word, he tucked her arm into his and together, they skated back.

When Carolyn and David saw them, they called, "Do you want a ride up?"

Andy glanced at Gina and knew she needed more time. "No, we'll climb the hill. The exercise will be good for us."

The clock struck eleven. In each other's arms on the sofa before the fire, Dan murmured, "I've got to go. We have a big day tomorrow."

"Must you?" Cindy replied.

"You know I do." Standing, Dan went over to the kitchen. "I presume all these cans contain good things to eat. Can I take them to the clinic now?"

Grateful that she wouldn't have to lug them over herself, she said, "Sure, I'll help you take them out." And so they loaded the SUV.

Turning to Cindy before he got in the SUV, Dan said, "I know we have a lot to talk about. I suspect we're both going to be busy tomorrow. You're getting ready for the open house and I'm out of town at a clinic way north of Algonquin Park. I made the commitment months ago or I'd cancel it. It's a long drive there and back. It will probably be after eleven when I get in."

Taking her in his arms, he said, "I'll miss you. Try not too work too hard tomorrow. We'll go somewhere Saturday after the open house and have a nice leisurely meal and talk."

"Drive carefully tomorrow," Cindy said. "I'll see you bright and early Saturday."

As he disappeared down the lane, Cindy couldn't help think that Fate was trying to keep them apart for yet a little longer.

The morning of the open house, Cindy arrived at the clinic at eight along with her students. Dan was there ready to assist her. He helped her put her materials in his kitchen and then dragged her into his office. "I suppose you're going to be with those students and food all day," he grumbled as he pulled her into his arms.

Running her hands over his jaw line and up behind his ears, she teased, "Oh, I might be able to find a moment here and there for you." Then she pulled his head down. Their kiss was long and satisfactory. Coming up for breath, they were going to squeeze in another kiss when Merry walked in. Flustered, she excused herself.

Holding Cindy tightly for one last moment, Dan said, "I can't believe that, at last, we're together. It seems to good to be true."

Breaking away and opening the door, Cindy called over her shoulder, "Believe it."

Cindy was touched when the most exquisite flower

setting arrived. Gina placed it on the reception counter with a sign that said *Catering by Cindy Howard* and insisted that Cindy wear a badge saying *Cindy Howard, Catering*. When Cindy objected that she was not a catering company, Gina said it was worth her job if Cindy didn't wear it. Then she'd surprised Cindy by producing some business cards Dan had made just in case she got inquiries.

The open house was a great success. As early as eleven, people started to trickle in and by one in the afternoon, the students and Cindy could barely keep up with the crowd. Cindy figured word had spread quickly and a lot of last-minute Christmas shoppers were taking a lunch break at the same time they were checking out the facilities. It didn't matter. It was all good public relations for Dan and Merry.

Cindy had brought Sweet Pea knowing that she would enjoy all the attention. She wasn't wrong. The sociable little calico was everywhere, up on the counter by the flowers, riding around on a technician's shoulder and rubbing against the legs of those sitting while they tasted the special little items Cindy had added to her sandwiches; miniature egg rolls, tiny pizzas the children loved and delectable toasts with smoked salmon.

Crash was a great hit. His cage was on a table in the hall that led to the examining rooms. The children could watch him as he played with a toy or suddenly flopped into a puppy snooze. They were interested in his bandages so Dan quickly assigned the technician to answer their questions. By four o'clock when the last visitor left, Cindy had had several inquiries about catering jobs. Not sure of her plans yet, Cindy had given out her parents' phone number.

The students assisted Cindy to pack the extra food

into parcels which she left in Dan's freezer. Then, they helped clean up any equipment they'd used and lastly, Cindy paid them.

Dan was coming along the hall by Crash's cage when Gina said, "Hal Martin wants to talk to you." Not tonight, Dan thought as he headed into reception to take the call. His heart sank when he heard Hal say, "I'm sorry, Dan, I need you out here. One of the Jerseys is in trouble." Dan groaned. Hal's Jerseys were incredibly valuable. He continued, "It's Belinda. She's having a breech birth and the calf is huge. It could be she'll need a caesarean." Dan said he would come and hung up.

Finding Cindy, he explained about Belinda, the prized Jersey. "I'll have to cancel supper, I'm afraid. This could go on all night and maybe part of tomorrow. There is always the chance the mother could suffer hypocalcemia. I'll have to stay until I'm sure both are safe and stabilized. Look, I'll phone you in the morning when I'm sure how things are going."

Taking her in his arms and kissing her, he said ruefully, "You see how it will be when you marry a veterinarian."

She hugged him tightly to her and said, "Take care. I want you back in one piece. And tell Belinda to get on with things."

Chuckling at that, Dan grabbed his coat and case and left.

Bursting with unexpected energy, Cindy tracked down Sweet Pea and put her in her cage, locked up and headed for the car. Although she'd been sure of Dan's intentions, they'd had so little time together uninterrupted that they had not discussed their future. But Dan had said "marry" and her heart lifted at the thought.

Chapter Seven

Cindy was wakened by the phone the next morning. Squinting at the clock, she saw that it was almost nine. It was Dan and he sounded absolutely exhausted. "The cow and calf have finally settled down and seem safe to leave but it was a rough night," he told her. "I had to do a caesarean and then monitor the cow and calf until just a little while ago. I want to see you Cindy, but I think I have to go home and sleep first. How about supper at the falls about five?"

Yawning, Cindy agreed and suggested he meet her there. Hanging up, she turned over, intending to sleep a little more but she found she was wide awake. She decided to have breakfast and then go for a walk along the lake. The ice was still clear but the weather on the radio promised warmer temperatures and snow later that night. She decided to take her camera too, to record the clarity of the ice and the sand and stones beneath.

169

Picking up the local paper, Cindy checked through the advertisements. It was Sunday and she was sure there would be a special candlelight service in several of the churches. Sure enough, the church she had attended all her life had one beginning at seven that evening. Maybe they both could attend.

As she changed into heavy clothes for her walk along the shore, she made two other decisions. First she had no intention of doing any work when she returned. Instead she would relax and read a book and get ready to meet Dan. Then, she'd go into town early and peek into the store windows. Maybe she'd see the puppy. Around four she'd watch the sun set on the falls. After that she'd meet Dan in the restaurant.

Cindy had just reached the bridge over the falls when she heard someone say, "Would you look at what the Russell twins are up to now." She looked across the falls toward the limestone ledges and the fishing dock just in time to see two youngsters about ten years of age running along the dock pursuing a spot of yellow. It was the puppy. The boys came to a halt when the puppy jumped up on the forbidden ledge and began to make her way along it. She could see the boys yelling at the pup, their mouths moving and their arms waving. That frightened the puppy even more and it crawled along until it could go no further.

Cindy rushed back to her car and called Dan. To her relief he answered. "Dan," she said. "You need to get over to the falls as soon as possible. The other puppy is out on the ledge that we used to jump from. Those monkeys, the Russell twins, chased it there. Call 911. I'm going out to see if I can coax it back to the dock."

With that, she hung up and opened her trunk. In it was a half a bag of kitty litter she kept to give her traction on ice and a box of dry cat food she'd picked up for Sweet Pea only minutes before. Opening the box, she took off one of her mitts and filled it with treats. She put more in her left pocket. Grabbing the kitty litter and slamming the trunk, she headed over the bridge.

Dan heard the phone click off even before it quite registered what Cindy had said. Then the image of her on that ledge filled his mind and he exploded into action. First he phoned Doc Anderson.

When the doctor answered, Dan said, "Jim. I've got a real emergency."

"What's up?" asked the doctor dryly. "Your beloved hurt herself again?"

"I'll tell you what's up. My beloved is, as we speak, preparing to go out on that ledge at the falls where the kids jump in the summer. She plans to rescue that puppy that's been wandering around town."

"I see. I don't suppose she had the sense to put on a life jacket."

"No, I'm sure she wouldn't. But thanks for suggesting it. I have some here. Look, Jim. You climb in the summer. Could you bring over some equipment? I'm going to try to get out on that ledge and inject the puppy so he's quiet. Then we'll try to get a life jacket on him and you can hoist him up. Maybe you'll have to hoist us up, too. Phone 911, will you and explain what's happening."

"Before you hang up," the doctor said, "give me your cell phone number." They exchanged numbers and Dan hung up.

Collecting two adult life jackets, a pet jacket and the necessary injection, Dan hurried out to the SUV and headed to the falls. The phone rang and the doctor said, "You'll be glad to know that someone has called 911 already and that indeed, Cindy is out on that ledge."

Dan didn't know whether to cuss or pray so he did both.

It was still light enough to see into the sides of the whirlpool and along the chasm walls when he arrived. Dan didn't waste time checking to see where Cindy was. There were enough people hanging over the bridge and looking out from the restaurant verandah to assure him she was right where she said she would be.

Dan already had his life jacket on. When he saw how icy the ledge was, he decided he could only manage with the small jacket for the puppy looped over his arm. Noticing that there was no sight of the twins, he turned to a watching teenager. "Do you know Doctor Anderson?"

The kid nodded.

"Good," said Dan. "Take this extra jacket up to him as soon as he arrives and tell him that I could only carry the small one."

Then without wasting any more time, Dan took out his Swiss Army knife, opened it so the blade was extended and knelt down to crawl along the ledge.

Cindy lay flat out on the ledge, her inside arm extended and in her hand, the part bag of litter from which she trickled it for traction. Her outside hand gripped the icy edge of the limestone for stability. Finally, she got as near the puppy as she dared. No longer needing the litter, she let the plastic bag drop into the churning waters below.

Those watching saw something flutter down and a cry went up but all that Cindy heard was the roar of the huge wall of water plunging down ahead of her, throwing up mist and wetting her face. The puppy had turned around now and was crunched down on her tummy, visibly trembling. Cindy still had her mitten full of cat treats tucked up her sleeve. Praying that the motion wouldn't frighten the little beast, she gingerly brought her hand away from the edge and, with trembling fingers, pulled the mitten out.

She lay still with her face down on her hands after that to rest for a moment. She tried blowing on her one exposed hand to warm it. Ignoring the noise of the falls and the slipperiness of the ledge, she shook out some of the treats before her and tried to push them with her freezing fingers toward the pup.

Finally, some rolled near enough that the puppy either caught the scent of the treats or was curious enough to edge toward them. She held her breath and waited. A moment later, the pup eased himself forward and managed to lap some up with its tongue.

She shook some more out and pushed them out only a little way. Cautiously, the puppy nibbled his way nearer. If only she could get him to take some out of her hand. She shook the last out on the ledge and with fingers so cold she could hardly manage, she picked up the bits of food and held them in her open hand.

She could feel herself beginning to tremble with cold now. She was sure the puppy would see the movement. She closed her eyes and prayed. Suddenly, she felt the raspy wetness of the puppy's tongue. Holding her breath again until the pup tried to get the last tidbit, Cindy grabbed the puppy and pulled him against her face and shoulders. The puppy began to struggle. At that moment, Cindy felt a pair of hands grip her waist.

Dan. She knew it was Dan without even looking.

She felt him shift his weight so he was partly on her. Then he reached around her shoulder and touched her cheek.

She nodded at his unspoken question. She felt him ease himself up a little farther and then he called above the noise of the falls, "I'm going to reach over your head and try to give the puppy an injection so he'll stop wriggling."

Clutching the struggling puppy as tightly as possible, she kept still as he reached around her. She felt him strain forward and then relax. "Got her," he shouted. "Give her five minutes." Then he eased back and waited. Finally, Cindy felt the skinny little body go limp.

At that moment, spotlights suddenly flooded the face of the chasm. Cindy was aware of bits of ice and stone tumbling down. Seconds later, she found herself looking into the face of Doc Anderson as he hung suspended from a rope.

He looked the scene over carefully and then moved along the ledge toward Dan. He reached for the puppy's life jacket and slipped it off Dan's arm. Swinging back to Cindy, he maneuvered the puppy into the jacket and velcroed it tightly. Then he tied a rope that hung from above through the loop on the back of the jacket and pulled on the rope twice. Someone above hauled the limp little beast up.

With the puppy gone, Cindy was aware that Dan now had a strong grip around her waist again. She was wondering just what she should do next when the line came back with a long yellow object she recognized as a water skier's waist floatation device. The doctor unclipped it and pushed it against her waist where Dan's hands were. She lifted her body as well as she could as the doctor slid the belt beneath her and fastened it around her. Then, he indicated they should begin to crawl back.

Now that her attention was not on the puppy, Cindy became shockingly aware of the frothing water only a few feet below her. As she tried to slide back, she felt the smoothness of ice as it built up along the ledges and realized now that the sun had disappeared, a layer of ice would coat the entire side of the wall of the chasm in no time. Visions of sliding into the water crept into her imagination and for a moment she felt completely paralyzed with fear. Her entire body trembled with cold and anxiety.

She felt Dan strain over her again and his hand touch her cheek softly. She touched his hand and her control returned. Together they began to wriggle back, the doctor always close to them, his hand on the ledge forming a barrier from the depths below. Finally, they reached the end of the ledge and the concrete dock.

Strong hands lifted first Dan and then Cindy into upright positions on the dock and the doctor swung in beside them. A cheer went up from all those watching but neither Cindy nor Dan heard the sound. Instead, Dan grabbed Cindy by the shoulders and said, "If you ever do something that stupid again, I'll—"

He never finished. Cindy cried, "Dan Hamilton. Shut up and kiss me."

Across at the restaurant and along the bridge, the crowd cheered as they watched the two of them embrace. Jason Bright, the high-school photographer, caught them in his close-up lens and captured their kisses forever while his classmate Darcy Dabrinsky zeroed in with her video recorder with a smile of satisfaction. Finally, the doctor tapped each of them on the shoulder and yelled, "Get up that hill and into my car. I want to check you over."

"The puppy?" asked Cindy.

"The new veterinarian came along just as I was about to descend. She said she'd look after it. Now, move it, and no more canoodling."

Along the bridge two Cupids cheered and threw their arms around each other. "They really have made up, they're still kissing," they crowed, ignoring the fact that it was the puppies that had really created the miracle.

Henry, staff advisor for the school yearbook, urged Jason to get his photos developed in a hurry and contact a wire service. He suggested Darcy offer her footage of the rescue to the TV station in Smithboro for the ten o'clock news.

Jim Anderson drove toward the animal clinic rather than his office. But did his passengers notice? he thought wryly. Not a chance. They were still wrapped together tighter than a taped rib, whispering and kissing.

He wheeled into the clinic driveway and said, "Okay, you two. Quit the smooching."

Amused at their confusion when they realized the car had stopped, he added, "I don't need to check you over, I just wanted to give you some privacy. However, if you can stop kissing long enough to go inside, I will look at your hand, Cindy, and assure myself that there is no frostbite. Although," he added with a smirk, "how that could possibly happen is hard to imagine. The two of you have steamed up my back windows."

Satisfied that he had their attention, he got out of the car and opened the back door. "Hurry up."

Even then, in spite of all his teasing, they couldn't keep their hands off each other. Dan had his arm around Cindy and was guiding her into the clinic as if she was a precious piece of china. Ah, the doctor thought with a sigh of satisfaction. Ain't love grand.

Of course, the first thing they had to do was check the puppy. Merry had wrapped the puppy up in a warm blanket and was just placing her in a cage lined with hot-water bottles. "I was going to get Peter in here," she explained, "but he must have been out at the falls with the rest of the population. Anyway, this little one is a real cutie. I'll stay and keep an eye on her."

Having let the two lovers satisfy themselves that the puppy was okay, the doctor marched them into Dan's office. Once they had their coats off, he said, "Okay, Cindy, let's see your hand."

As he checked it for frostbite, he asked, "Why on earth did you take off your glove?"

Cindy flexed her fingers, happy that they'd stopped hurting. "I had a box of cat food in the car. I was afraid I wouldn't be able to get the contents out without frightening the puppy or worse still, moving too much and slipping off the ledge. I decided to stuff the food into my mitt and stick it up my sleeve." With a shrug, she added, "It worked."

"Well," the doctor said, "Your hand seems fine. However, while you're here, I might as well take out your stitches. Dan, close your eyes. This isn't going to hurt her as you know. But I'd just as soon not take a chance of you swooning."

Dan closed his eyes. He just didn't trust his stomach when he thought of scissors and Cindy's hand. "You're enjoying this, aren't you Jim?"

"Absolutely."

"Just you wait," Dan said, "your turn will come and then we'll see who's laughing."

Ignoring Dan, the doctor took out the stitches. Then

he said, "As far as I can see, neither of you seem any the worse for your adventure." He couldn't resist adding, "I would be relieved, Dan, if in the future you could keep your damsel out of trouble."

With a predictably dreamy look on his face, Dan put his arm around Cindy's shoulders and said, "I intend to try."

"I'm off. I was just going to sit down to supper."

Prying himself from Cindy's side, Dan said, "Thanks Jim. I don't think we could have made it if you hadn't climbed down and helped."

The doctor was heading for the door when the phone rang. He paused while Dan answered. The call might be for him. One of his patients was due to deliver any day.

Dan listened for a moment, and then said, "You'd better stick around. That was the high-school yearbook team. They're begging for an interview. Seems they've sold our story and have a deadline to meet. I don't have the nerve to turn them down. Henry would never forgive me if I discouraged his protégées."

Bowing to the inevitable, they headed to Dan's apartment for coffee and the interview.

Dan shifted his arm so that Cindy could tuck herself up against him as they watched the ten o'clock news in front of the fire. "I wonder exactly what Darcy caught on that video of hers," Cindy said.

Brushing a curl back from her cheek, Dan said, "I hope it was just the rescue but knowing the media, I have a feeling there'll be more."

Just then, the words 'Stewart's Falls' caught their attention. Suddenly, the falls appeared. Darcy had done a good job. Her first shot showed the falls up close, the power of the water very evident as it surged over the precipice. Then she had panned across to the face of the chasm walls. Starting at the top, she took the viewer down, ledge by ledge, until the camera caught Cindy struggling with her mitt and then holding her hand out.

Recalling the moment, Cindy shivered and Dan pulled her closer to his side.

Darcy focused in on the puppy and Cindy's hand, arm and head. She caught the puppy's fear and then its hunger as it finally wiggled its small body toward Cindy's hand. When the puppy finally touched Cindy's hand, Darcy's recorder caught the sounds of those watching over the roar of the falls.

The next shot showed Dan reaching over Cindy. Again the recorder caught the voices of those watching: "What's he doing?" "Is he going to take the puppy?" "Won't he drop it?" "I think he gave it an injection."

Darcy showed Doc Anderson slipping down the rope to the three on the ledge and the ascent of the semiconscious puppy. Switching back to Dan and Cindy, she followed their movements as they wriggled back toward safety with the doctor hovering in front of them.

But what must have been the biggest moment of Darcy's young career was the kiss. "Oh, Dan," Cindy giggled and hid her face on his shoulder. "The whole world saw me throw myself into your arms. I'll never live it down."

Peeking back over her shoulder at the TV screen, she added, "And that has to be the longest kiss in TV history."

Clicking off the TV, Dan turned to her and took her face in his hands. Kissing her forehead, her eyes, her lips, he murmured, "I love you, Cindy Howard. I want to marry you, to make a home with you and have a family with you. But I also want you to achieve your dreams. Is there any way we can both have our dreams come true?"

Cindy couldn't help it. Tears flooded her eyes. She gave him a watery smile and whispered, "Maybe I could have a tearoom as well as love you, marry you and have our children."

"Ah, sweetheart. For a moment, I thought you were going to say you had to go away. I think a tearoom would be wonderful. What about Alice's house?"

Cindy's eyes sparkled with enthusiasm. "I've thought of nothing else for the last few days. I'm sure we could do it."

Dan got up and put another log on the fire. Returning to the sofa, he said, "Now, let's plan our future."

Chapter Eight

Carolyn and David stood at their door, wishing their guests goodnight. She sighed happily. Turning into her husband's arms, she said, "This has been the most marvelous Christmas Day. Thank you so much for my presents."

Just then, a thin little bundle of yellow fur trotted toward them, a soft toy in her mouth. Carolyn knelt down. "Come here, Lucy."

"Lucy?" said David.

"Yup. Lucy." Carolyn picked up the wiggling puppy, kissed her and straightened her red bow. "She's lovely. It's amazing how she's come along. Merry said the minute she cuddled up to Crash, she stopped being nervous."

Giving David a smug little smile, she said, "Let's go and see what our lovers have to say for themselves. They've managed to evade our attention for two days. And Cindy changed the subject every time I tried to

181

find out what had happened between them while we made dinner."

Giving her a peck on her Cupid's nose, he said, "That's because they don't need our help anymore."

Cindy and Dan were curled up on one of the sofas before the fire with Crash asleep at the other end when the two Cupids came in. "Okay," said Carolyn. "You've kept us waiting long enough."

"Waiting for what?" Dan asked innocently.

Cindy laughed and gave him a poke. "Quit teasing them. Sit down and we'll tell you our plans."

Cindy opened her mouth to speak when Carolyn suddenly squealed, "You're engaged. When did this happen? You didn't have a ring earlier."

They answered together. "Just now."

"So?" Carolyn demanded.

"So," said Dan, "We're going to have a quiet wedding when Cindy finishes school. We talked to her parents last night and they were delighted."

"And . . . ?" said David.

Smiling blissfully at Dan, Cindy answered, "We're going to open a tearoom in Alice Thornton's house. Dan talked to Alice Monday morning. We both went to the bank yesterday. I have to bring in a business plan but they seem interested."

Dan added, "For the first few months, we're going to live at the clinic. When the tearoom takes off, we're going to fix up the second floor and live there until we need more space."

"What about the house you'd planned?" asked Carolyn. "Will you sell the lot?"

Dan shook his head. "Once we're sure that we can manage the tearoom, we'll build the house. What's made it all possible is the fact that Merry is sure she wants to join the practice. Her share will give us sufficient funds to get the tearoom started and, in time, to build the house."

Carolyn leaned back against David and said with satisfaction, "Everything has worked out wonderfully. You two have finally seen the light. We're giving Lucy and Crash a home. And lastly, Merry has decided to settle in Stewart's Falls."

Just then, Charlie the cat came wandering in, sniffed the sleeping pup and jumped up on Dan's lap.

"You have to admit that Charlie is a superior cat. He's absolutely cool around the puppies," David said with pride.

"Something else good happened," said Dan. "Merry met Ruth and her little boy and she has hired Ruth as a housekeeper and nanny. She worried that doing both was asking too much of Ruth but Ruth was so glad to be able to spend her time with her son that she convinced Merry to give it a try."

Carolyn yawned. "It's been a long day. I've had it. I'm off to bed as soon as I put the puppies in their cage." Pulling David to his feet, she said to Dan and Cindy, "You two come up whenever you want. You know where to go."

Putting down an indignant Charlie, Dan said to Cindy, "Let's turn in now. It's been an exhausting two or three days. And who knows, I could still be called out."

Putting the puppies to bed wasn't as hard as anticipated. As long as Lucy could snuggle in with Crash, she was content. "It's a good thing you bought a large cage," Carolyn observed. "I think Crash and Lucy will use it together for a long time."

"You're happy with your present?" asked David.

"I love them. Even Charlie isn't too concerned

about them." Putting an arm around his waist, she said, "Come on, I'm exhausted."

Charlie remained in the kitchen, his tail switching slightly as he watched the sleeping puppies. He helped himself to some of their kibble and then, with tail held high, headed for the family room and the Christmas tree. For a few minutes, he rustled around among the presents, nosing into bags and pouncing on tissue. A bright red ball hanging on a low limb caught his attention. Enthusiastically, he batted it back and forth until it fell to the floor. Unable to resist, he chased it back and forth until it rolled under a sofa.

Not quite tired out, he returned to the tree and studied it. A pair of frosted glass Cupids, fused together in flight, their arrows on the ready, hung just above his head. Carefully, he stood up on his haunches and delicately snagged them with his paw. Chrr-ing with pleasure, he picked them up in his mouth. Spotting a box with a soft blue sweater tucked under the tree, he settled in it, his chin resting on his Cupid prize.